Harley
THE K9 FILES

Dale Mayer

HARLEY: THE K9 FILES, BOOK 14
Beverly Dale Mayer
Valley Publishing Ltd.

ISBN-13: 978-1-773364-40-7
Print Edition

Books in This Series

Ethan, Book 1
Pierce, Book 2
Zane, Book 3
Blaze, Book 4
Lucas, Book 5
Parker, Book 6
Carter, Book 7
Weston, Book 8
Greyson, Book 9
Rowan, Book 10
Caleb, Book 11
Kurt, Book 12
Tucker, Book 13
Harley, Book 14
Kyron, Book 15
Jenner, Book 16
Rhys, Book 17
Landon, Book 18
Harper, Book 19
Kascius, Book 20
Declan, Book 21
Bauer, Book 22
Delta, Book 23
Conall, Book 24
Baron, Book 25
Walton, Book 26

Boxed Sets and Bundles
https://geni.us/Bundlepage

About This Book

Welcome to the all new K9 Files series reconnecting readers with the unforgettable men from SEALs of Steel in a new series of action packed, page turning romantic suspense that fans have come to expect from USA TODAY Bestselling author Dale Mayer. Pssst… you'll meet other favorite characters from SEALs of Honor and Heroes for Hire too!

Returning to the town he was raised in was hard, except that Harley can once more see the only golden light of those days. He'd walked away from her because she'd been too young, and he would never be good enough. Harley was back to check on the War Dog Bowser, but Harley can't help but feel like he never really left. But when Harley snags the War Dog from one of Bowser's handlers, Harley knows he has to put a stop to this guy forever.

Over all these years Jasmine awaits Harley's return, but he won't be happy with the changes she's gone through. When he shows up out of the blue, she knows only complete honesty will be good enough. But it was rough and meant opening up memories of a horrible time in her life.

Harley's arrival prompts a hidden truth that someone will do anything to stop from coming out. And Harley will do everything he can to get justice for her …

Sign up to be notified of all Dale's releases here!

https://geni.us/DaleNews

PROLOGUE

HARLEY BERTRAM WALKED into Badger's office. Geir and Erick were also there with Badger. Harley slumped into the chair, only to wince, and shifted his position.

"How are the injuries these days?" Erick asked.

"Much better than I expected." Harley rotated his right wrist, then his left—a prosthetic. "Some of the surgeries did better than others."

"But you're handling the hammer just fine."

"And the keyboards are getting easier too. So what's up? Cade said that you were looking for me."

"Any dog experience?"

Harley shrugged. "Outside of the fact that I love them, no."

"No K9 experience in the military?" Badger asked.

"Assisting with the War Dogs, yes, but I never had my own. I worked with the training groups." He sighed. "Man, they were good animals."

Erick nodded. "Have you heard about the War Dogs that we've been trying to locate and to help?"

Harley frowned and shook his head. "I don't know how I missed that because, honest to God, it's hard to miss anything in this place."

"True enough." Cade walked into the room, with a folder. He tossed it on the table in front of Badger. "I'm not sure what we'll do with this one."

"I don't know either." Badger nodded. "I read it early this morning."

"Read what?" Harley asked.

"So this is Bowser, a male War Dog. He was adopted and then sold."

"Isn't that against the terms of service in the adoption contract?"

"It absolutely is, but they didn't seem to care."

"What was he sold for?"

"As a security dog," he replied.

"Well, that might not be such a bad life."

"Maybe, except it looks like he's in a possible grow op."

"Oh no, not drugs. Those people treat the animals really rough."

"Exactly," Badger agreed. "So we want to make sure the dog's being well treated, and, if it's not, to remove him from the situation."

"But, if they bought and paid for Bowser, they might not take too kindly to that suggestion."

"He's the property of the United States government. Adoptions are done on the basis where you are looking after the War Dog but do not get to own one."

"Right, and if I get any resistance?"

The four men looked at him.

"Ah, so doesn't matter what kind of resistance there is. I have a job to do."

"Exactly." Badger cocked his head. "Unless you got a problem with that."

"Hell no," Harley countered. "The fewer rules, the better. Whereabouts?"

"Montana. He's set up near the Canadian border."

Harley frowned. "I wouldn't have thought the drug-running business or the cannabis business was really good up there."

"Well, that's why we've got a question mark on it. I'm not exactly sure what you'll find there. But hopefully you'll find our War Dog is a security dog in that location."

"And legally sold, as far as the current owners know. That could be a bit tough. Any money to help buy back the dog?"

"Some, it just depends on what kind of money we're talking about."

"Right." He stood. "And when do I go?"

"The sooner, the better. The locals contacted the War Dog department about the dog because another one showed up dead."

"Another War Dog?"

"No, another dog and then they heard about this one, so they were asking if it was the same one."

"And the answer, of course, is no."

"I think they were also warning the War Dog department that the particular dog had been abused."

"*Great*," Harley muttered under his breath. "Do I get to carry weapons too?"

"What do you want?" Badger asked, with interest.

Harley reached out and flexed his hand. "I have a couple of my own."

"I'll get the permits," Badger confirmed, "for travel. I don't want you to go up against a cartel or some such thing without firepower."

"The dog hasn't been there all that long," Cade noted. "You might get it on your side and turn it against its owners."

"You know what the answer is for that then," Harley muttered. "The drug-runners will just end up shooting it."

"In that case why don't you just shoot the drug-runners," Cade suggested in a rough voice. "We've seen so many bad assholes in this world, but I get really pissed off when somebody hurts an animal."

Harley stood, heading for the door. "I hear you. I'll check it out and let you know what I find." Harley stopped and looked back at Badger's team. "Did you guys know that I spent ten years in Montana?" The men looked at him in surprise. He smiled. "I guess not."

"When were you there?"

"I was a foster kid. I left because I was getting too attached to the family. It seemed like a good idea at the time. I turned eighteen and joined the navy. The history after that you know well."

"What do you mean, *too attached*?" Badger asked curiously.

He nodded. "The foster family was not okay, but their daughter was dynamite." And, with a wicked grin, he turned and walked out.

Badger called back. "Have you kept in touch with them?"

"No. I guess I will now though."

"What's her name?"

Harley laughed as he stuck his face back into the room. "Jasmine. She was the sweetest little thing. Although I wouldn't say that to her face." He shook his head. "She is just as likely to shoot me on sight right now."

"Why's that?" Badger frowned at him. "Maybe we shouldn't send you."

"It's all good," Harley replied. "She wanted me to stay,

and I didn't dare."

"Why?" Cade asked.

"Her family. I wasn't good enough," he explained. "Believe me. I won't be good enough now either."

"Maybe they've changed," Erick suggested.

"Maybe." Harley shrugged. "But I haven't."

CHAPTER 1

LOOKING IN MONTANA for a dog named Bowser was hardly something Harley had thought would be part of his life. Yet returning to this part of the world was a goal that he'd never really left behind, because Jasmine had been here. What did one do with that first love that never had a chance to go anywhere?

Eureka, Montana, was a place where he had spent, as he had told Badger and the others, ten years. He'd arrived as a desperate, young, broken-hearted boy who'd lost his grandmother—the only loving family member he had. He shook his head, as he drove through the town. A lot of this area had grown more than he had expected. But then his memories were from a while ago. He had a lot of good memories here, but most of the memories were of his childhood with his grandmother and then growing up in a foster home, where he felt included and accepted by the daughter, Jasmine, but never accepted by the foster parents. There'd always been that sense of *You're here only temporarily.*

It wasn't his home. It would never be his home.

It wasn't a family he had kept in touch with after he left. It had been made very clear that he was for optics, not because they were good people or that they were doing their best and that this was the way they could be of service. They weren't the kind of people who wanted to adopt him or to keep him around long-term, particularly not once a relationship between him and Jasmine developed. That had been something they'd been against from the very beginning and had let him know in no uncertain terms that their daughter was off-limits.

Harley hadn't understood anything except rejection. It had been something he'd struggled with for a long time. And, at one point in time, it had made life difficult because he was trying to find his own feet, and that rejection had hurt. But, when his foster parents had made it very clear that they would dump his ass back into the foster system, and he could finish his school wherever, he had toned it down and had stayed quiet and acted "decent" per their rules, just to graduate from high school, just to reach the age of majority.

But he hadn't forgotten.

And twelve years later, he wanted to say that he'd forgiven the harsh treatment by his foster parents, but, at the same time, he wasn't exactly sure what was the right way to deal with the residual effects from that couple either. They were obviously terrified that Harley would take their daughter down the wrong path and then leave her in a bad way. He certainly had cared enough about her—and he had believed at the time that Jasmine had truly cared about him—but there was no getting away from the fact that her parents hated that the two would have anything to do with each other.

Even now Harley was both excited and unnerved at the thought of seeing Jasmine again. He had no wish to see the rest of the family. He wasn't the man he was when he left, and that was a good thing because that version of him had toned down things to get by, and that had served him well in the military. It had given him patience and endurance and the ability to bite his tongue.

There had been plenty of opportunities in the military where Harley had really wanted to let loose, but being court-martialed for bad behavior wasn't something that he wanted to encounter. The navy had punishments that went over and above anything that his foster family could have devised.

As it was, Harley had left, telling Jasmine that he would return but, of course, hadn't. His good-bye speech had been only to stop her tears and to get out of a situation he knew had no happy ending—especially if she wasn't prepared to leave with him. But then, she'd only been sixteen, and that had been even harder for him to deal with over each passing day because he had been older. He'd wanted to take that further step with her but didn't out of respect for her and his foster family. He also knew that step would lead to an ending of which there was no going back from, at least from her parents' perspective.

Harley had left as soon as he could to avoid that attraction. And, of course, Jasmine, being sixteen, had desperately wanted him to promise to come back, so he had. But he knew at the time that he wasn't returning, and he figured she'd known it too, even at sixteen. But, if not then, now, some twelve years later, she should be more than happy that he had left. Or at least that she had had a full life that she wouldn't have had if he had stuck around.

The best thing Harley could have done was go into the navy, but he didn't want to tell his foster family that—although they probably figured it was a good thing because it got him out of their hair. Plus it would straighten him out because, as far as they were concerned, he needed straightening out. Yet what he really needed was acceptance and a little love, and that was in short supply with this temporary family. With that foster family came lots of discipline, lots of anger, and lots of *You will do this because we say so.*

But, at the same time, they gave him food, a bed, and a roof over his head. That the home environment had been cold and that the foster parents didn't include him was a completely different issue. Harley didn't understand his foster parents' desire to have a foster child around. Harley couldn't envision *needing* a foster child around, especially when his foster parents had no healthy feelings toward him.

Plus, they had a child. A biological child. It's not like Harley filled a childless gap in their home. He shook his head at the thought. He didn't know what kind of sin his foster parents were trying to make up for or what kind of life they were trying to give anybody because, from Harley's perspective, it had been a pretty rough one right from the get-go. He felt sure Jasmine would agree with him, even today.

But Harley had survived, and he had to admit it was in part because of them. So they deserved his respect if nothing else. He never talked to anybody about the kind of relationship he had with them—even not telling Jasmine much, as they were her birth parents—yet the saving grace for all of the dysfunction in that household had been Jasmine. As a little sister, she'd been to die for. The fact that she wasn't his sister had just added to their stress and their relationship issues.

As far as his foster family was concerned, he would never be good enough, and he needed to learn that lesson right off the bat. And he did. The foster parents didn't hold back right from the beginning, so, when Harley realized how close he and Jasmine were getting, he knew it would just be trouble. When somebody was off-limits at that stage, off-limits was off-limits. No such thing as partial off-limits. It was like, *You are a bad deal, Harley. Get out of here fast, before you break our rules, … before you cross these lines.*

He drove through Eureka, staring at the relatively large malls that had sprung up since he'd been gone. He even passed what looked like a large training center, maybe for the sheriff or the military. He shook his head in wonder and kept on going. As he traveled through the town, heading north, he realized that he hadn't given the location much credence, when he thought about the drug-running and the problem of the dog. Eureka was very close to the Canadian border, just about nine miles farther north. Maybe that was good, as far as drug-running went. Maybe they were crossing the border all the time with the drugs. He didn't know.

Harley did know that a pub was just on the outskirts. The family of an old friend of his owned the pub, and, as far as he knew at the time, his friend had gone into the family business and had no intention of ever leaving. They rented rooms over the pub, so Harley hoped to stay there and to see if his buddy was still around.

When the pub finally appeared in front of him, he smiled because, of all the things that made him feel like he'd come home, the pub was one of them. It didn't look any different. It still had great big antlers hanging above the entrance and still had a huge parking lot for truckers and God-only-knows whatever else. He wondered if they'd turned it into an RV park too, from the size of it and with how many RVs were there. Maybe they rented by the night there too.

Harley pulled off to the side, hopped out, and stretched his legs. The rental truck was fine, but after his injury—with a really bad parachuting accident, where he got winged midflight and crash-landed—his leg was never quite the same. Neither was his hip and, of course, his left arm. Still, he was way better than his buddies. One of them had not made it through that jump, and Harley swore he wouldn't argue or complain anymore. Yet human nature being what it was just made him do it anyway.

As he walked in through the double doors, he removed his sunglasses, stopped, and looked around. He swore to God that absolutely nothing was different in the place. Twelve years later and it looked like yesterday. He walked up to the front counter and sat down.

One of the help looked at him. "What will you have?"

"A plain burger and a beer," he replied instantly.

"Got it." Then he turned and walked away.

It had always been that way. Harley didn't need to look at the menu, didn't care to look at the menu. As long as it was still the same burger, he was good. When the barkeep returned with a draft in a tall glass, Harley smiled because that was the same too. He looked over at the bartender. "Any chance Daniel's around?"

His eyebrow lifted. "He's around here somewhere. He doesn't usually come on for another hour or so."

"Still likes night shift, does he?"

"Yeah, he does." The guy behind the counter studied Harley carefully. "You know him?"

"Yeah, we went to school together." Harley nodded.

"That's been a while ago."

"It has, indeed. But, if he's around, tell him Harley's here, will ya?"

"I think he's in the back. I'll see when I go get your burger."

"Good enough." Harley picked up the beer and took a

long drink. It was cold and refreshing. He wiped the foam off his mouth with the back of his hand and smiled because it was an actual movement he and Daniel had worked on and had perfected when they were in high school. Not that they should have been drinking back then, but, when your buddy was part of a bar, you got away with a little more than you should have.

Of course Harley had hoped his foster family hadn't noticed, but, knowing their direct lines into the gossip around this town, they probably had. Maybe that had further contributed to him not being desirable. Then he was somebody without connections, so he just wasn't desirable regardless. Made him sad to think about how, as a child, he'd been so harshly judged and found wanting. But he had certainly learned his lesson here.

And he'd also learned to keep his mouth shut and to keep his head down, as needed, which was pretty much 100 percent of the time. He'd grown up to be somebody who watched what was going on around him, took action when needed, but otherwise sidestepped a lot of trouble that could have come his way.

He enjoyed his beer, looking around, feeling old memories wash through him, but—with time and distance—they were mostly good memories. When the kitchen door opened again, and a huge monster of a man stepped out, his gaze scanning the front bar, he went past Harley and then zoomed back again.

The two men stared at each other for a long moment.

And then Daniel's face broke into a huge grin. He walked over and slapped Harley on the shoulder, who bounced to his feet and hugged the big man. "Damn, it's good to see you." Daniel studied Harley. "You're almost as big as me but not quite."

"Don't you look fine." Harley laughed. "Nobody's as big as you out here, except maybe your dad and your brother."

"Yep, they came pretty darn close, but I topped them both."

And there was just enough smugness to his tone that it made Harley laugh again. "Well, I'm glad to see that you beat them both out, since that was your goal."

"Yeah, that was me, he of high and lofty goals." He gave a hearty laugh. "Damn, it's good to see you. What the hell are you doing here?"

Just then the bartender returned with a burger. Daniel looked at it. "Just a plain burger, huh?"

"I didn't ask for a menu. This is the one that always brought back the memories."

"I forgot you didn't like pickles and all the rest of that stuff on your burger."

"Nope, I'm pure when it comes to my burgers—just meat and bun."

"I figured by now that surely you would have gotten a little more adventurous."

"Oh, I have," he agreed, "but this is the one thing that brings back the memories."

"Nothing wrong with that." He took the stool beside him. "What the hell are you doing here? I didn't think you'd ever come back."

"I wasn't planning on coming back either, but something came up, and I volunteered." His lips kicked up in the corners. "Surprised me too."

"Ha." Daniel snorted. "That family of yours, if they know you're here, they'll run you off."

"Why is that?" he asked, with a frown.

At that, Daniel stared at him, his eyebrow raised. "Because of your kid of course."

Harley froze. "What are you talking about?"

"What do you mean?" Daniel asked. "Don't … Surely you remember Jasmine?"

"Of course I remember Jasmine. Did she get pregnant?"

He stopped, looked at him. "It's yours, isn't it?"

"No, we never got to that stage. I wouldn't do that to her because I loved her. I wouldn't do that to her, what with her family. It's one of the reasons why I left as soon as I could because I knew I couldn't stop myself otherwise."

"Well, somebody else wasn't quite so willing to stop."

Harley stared at Daniel in shock. "And everyone thought it was mine?"

"Let's just say the timing was right."

He slowly shook his head. "It's not mine. That I know for sure."

"You're the only one who does." Daniel continued to stare him down. "I have to tell you that you probably shouldn't stick around town because both the townsfolk and the family's really got it in for you. Not that there's much family left."

"The child's not mine," he repeated in all seriousness.

Daniel looked him in the eye for a long moment. "Well, I believe you, I guess, because I got no reason not to trust you, but you know they won't believe you."

"Hell no, they won't." Harley's shoulders drooped, still stunned at this turn of events. "She said it was mine?"

Daniel's eyebrows shot up. "You know what? I'm not so sure that she did." Daniel considered that. "Not sure that anything she said would have been listened to because everybody jumped on the fact that you were the one who had left, and everybody knew the two of you had been sweet on each other."

"Sure, but that didn't mean that I'd have done that to her."

"Everybody thought the worst of you anyway. I mean, your son …" Then Daniel stopped and corrected himself. "Her son is eleven years old now. We're pretty darn sure she was pregnant when you left. If not then, it was within a week or two."

"And like I said," he murmured, "no way it's mine." Inside, he reeled from the shock. Had she been two-timing him the whole time? He'd been there, denying himself, doing everything he could to spare her, and instead she had been stepping out with somebody else? "I don't even know how to feel about that. Damn, it was killing me, but I was being so good."

"At least you have a clear conscience."

"And yet nobody here, of course, believes it." Harley shook his head. "Jesus."

"Regardless of that," Daniel added, "and we didn't expect you to come back. Why are you here?"

Harley snorted and filled him in.

"War Dogs." Daniel shook his head. "Not exactly sure I understand what all that's about."

"It was adopted in town and then sold to be a security dog."

"That's not too bad though, is it?"

"For a drug outfit."

At that, Daniel winced. "Well, we do have some bad drug-running that moved into town. … Well, not really into town. Just out of town. I've had a run-in with a couple of the guys myself a time or two."

"And they lived?" Harley asked in surprise. His friend's temper was legendary. As was his massive size.

"So far, and I have no wish to spend any time in jail myself," he noted, "but, if they keep pushing it, they'll get a little more than they asked for."

"I'm surprised they're causing trouble." Harley frowned. "That's not normal. Usually they want to keep a low profile."

"It's a couple assholes in the group." Daniel gave a one-arm shrug. "You know how it is. They think they're better than everybody and have to tell the world who they are."

"Only proving that, of course, they aren't even close." He nodded.

"You do understand guys like that."

"I spent twelve years in the navy. It's just amazing how different some people are."

"Are you sorry you went in?"

"Hell no. It was great. I learned a lot, changed a lot, became a man all on my own. The accident kind of screwed me over, but that wasn't their fault."

"No, and you were always a little bit more hell for leather anyway, so if you got injured on the job, that was probably you being a little too gung ho."

Harley burst out laughing. "How'd you know?" He smiled.

"Well, it's definitely who you are."

"It's who I was. I don't know about now."

"Good point." Daniel frowned. "Seriously, that's not your child?"

He looked at him and nodded. "Absolutely. It's not my child. And I have to tell you that it makes me feel pretty odd to think that that she was pregnant when I left because I had no idea."

"And you never had sex with her?"

"Nope, that was my agreement with her parents," he explained quietly. "And that's one promise I didn't break."

"And I think that's why they hate you so much."

"Does the son look anything like me?" he asked quietly.

Daniel shook his head. "No, he doesn't. Looks a lot like his mom though."

"Interesting," he murmured. He thought about it for a long time. "And I have no clue who the father would be either."

"Well, once the town finds out, you can bet there'll be an awful lot of speculation."

"Of course there will be. And there'll be a large group of them who won't believe what I'm saying no matter what."

"Probably not. I didn't know what to believe, having heard the rumors all these years, but honestly, I thought it was yours too."

"Of course you did, but then we were young smart-ass kids back then."

"And dying to get into every pair of pants we could." Daniel grinned.

"Well, you were certainly on that mission. I was just heading for the navy. I figured I'd get laid enough once I got in there."

At that, Daniel burst out laughing. "Isn't that the truth? I, on the other hand, was a good guy, and I got married."

"Wow. Who did you marry? Do I know her?"

"You sure do. I ended up marrying Diane."

He stopped and stared. "Pimply-faced, huge glasses, brainiac Diane?"

Again Daniel burst out laughing. "Absolutely. But you

should see her now. She finally grew up, grew out of that awkward stage, and blossomed."

"I'm really glad for you, … particularly if you're happy."

"Yep, we're very happy, and we got two boys." Daniel looked over at Harley. "You never did get married?"

"No, sure didn't." He paused. "Thought about it a time or two but never really could reconcile that relationship with how I felt about Jasmine."

"Still carrying a torch for her?"

"I was wondering about looking her up when I got here. Now I just feel really weird about it all because that means she was stepping out on me back then. Not something I wanted to hear."

"Sorry about that, dude. She's not the kind who I would have thought would do that either."

"No. So I'm not sure what happened." When Harley grew quiet, Daniel looked at him speculatively. Harley shook his head. "I mean it. I made a promise to the foster parents, and I never went against it. She was only sixteen. I made a promise to myself."

"Well, for what it's worth, I believe you. At least now I do."

"Now I have to wonder if I want to see her at all." Harley frowned. "You just dropped a bombshell on me."

"Well, you dropped one on me too." Daniel snorted. "On the other hand I'm still really glad to see you. Don't know about this War Dog stuff though. That sounds mighty upsetting, not how to treat a veteran, whether man or dog."

Daniel had always been a big baby when it came to animals. His family used to pick up all kinds of rescues. "Have you heard anything about a big shepherd-Malinois cross?"

"I have. One that was supposed to be quite dangerous. I

know that they found a dead dog on that supposed drug compound not too long ago. So I imagine that's caused a fair bit of talk."

"Absolutely. I can't imagine anything worse than for a man to abuse, much less kill a War Dog." Anger spiked in Harley's voice.

"I don't like people hurting animals, as you well know, but when they hurt an animal like that in such a ruthless way, it's just bad news."

"Once I get a place to sleep for the night, I'll take a drive out there and look at what I'm up against."

"Don't do that," Daniel said in alarm. "When I say that place is bad news, that means it's bad news. You let the authorities handle that one."

He snorted. "Well, the sheriff won't do a whole lot about this War Dog. That's why I'm here."

At that, his friend stared at him. "So what kind of work did you do in the navy?"

He gave a side tilt of his lips. "Stuff that handles these kinds of guys."

"Man, I don't like the idea of you going off and facing them," he said, frowning. "Especially not alone."

"I'll only take a look and check out the lay of the land first." He continued. "Per the parties, the dog may have been sold 'free and clear,' but it's still up to me to make sure it's taken care of properly. Particularly as this last sale was a breach of the government contract. If the animal is happy and well looked after, then fine, we won't interfere, until the next welfare check. However, if the dog's in anything but wonderful condition, that's not something I will tolerate."

"That's a whole different story. You know perfectly well that there can be food, and yet the animal's abused."

"I know, so I won't make any decisions until I see it."

"Still don't like anything about this." Daniel stared at his buddy, with a grim knowing look.

"Neither do I, but it was also an opportunity to come back here and stop in and visit."

"You could have done that without the dog rescue."

Harley grinned, lifted his glass, finished his beer, and called for another one. "You still rent rooms upstairs?"

"I do, but we're pretty full up. Let me see if there's a space." And, with that, Daniel got off the barstool and headed into the back.

Harley hoped there was a room available. He didn't need much, just a place to crash. It seemed so strange to think that Daniel had a wife and two kids. But, hey, he was happy. The big man had put on a lot of weight too, so his life was content, as he'd say.

Harley shied away from thinking about Jasmine having a child because that was just so wrong. For everybody to have thought it was his meant she'd had a relationship very fast, either before he left or right after. And that just made his stomach wrench open up into a deep pit. And wasn't that something after all these years, thinking his love for her had survived over a decade—and that hers had too. *Boy, was I wrong. And it hurt.*

Harley should have asked Daniel what she was doing for a living nowadays too and if the foster family was still around locally. He sat here, sipping his second beer, as he looked around. A couple people he thought he recognized, but he had hardly been a popular kid back then, so he wasn't exactly sure who people were. Just enough years had passed that it was hard to recognize anybody for sure.

When Daniel returned, he nodded. "I got one room for

you, but it's not fancy. It's not usually rented out."

"Does it have a bathroom?"

"It does. It's at the very back of the pub and small and barely furnished though."

"That's fine. I'll take it."

Daniel nodded. "I'd give you a room in the house with us, but, with the boys, there aren't any spare bedrooms."

"What will you do when child number three comes?" he asked.

At that, Daniel started to chuckle. "Well, number three is on its way"—he puffed up proudly—"so I'm not really sure what the answer to that question is."

"Wow. They're coming on hard and fast for you."

"Once you get into that family mode, it's easier just to have them right after each other, while you're still doing diaper duty."

"Diapers." He shook his head at that. "I just can't imagine you with diapers."

"None of that bothers me much. You know me. I was always up for getting dirty."

At that, Harley burst out laughing. That was positive evidence of marital bliss, even after all these years, and that Daniel was happy—when changing diapers was no big deal. Still grinning, Harley looked around at the place. "So much of this just looks like it hasn't been touched in all these years that I've been gone."

"It hasn't been. Dad's gone now though." Daniel gave his friend a sad smile. "Mom's okay, but she's sure showing her age too."

"I think it happens to all of us," Harley noted.

"It does, indeed." He tapped the bar. "Now that you had dinner, are you sticking around for the evening?"

"I'll take a drive through town." He shared a knowing look with his buddy. "Reacquaint myself with the layout."

"And stop in to see your ex?"

"Well, she's hardly my ex apparently," he noted quietly. "Where is she living now?"

"She's still at home." Then Daniel shook his head. "Of course you don't know."

"Know what?"

"Her dad was killed in a car accident, and her mom has dementia."

"Her mom's not very old."

"No, and it happened very quickly after the father's accident. I don't know if stress can bring on something like that but maybe."

"Ouch, that's a hard one for her."

"She's her mom's caregiver, so she's still at home."

"And that's not that easy either," he murmured. He nodded at his buddy, as he stood. "I'll stop by there later, when I've done my trip around town."

"You do that. Don't go to that drug compound though." He pointed a finger at him. "Certainly not in the dark."

"Why is that?" he asked curiously.

"I know they got electronic security, and they got dogs, but these are not dogs that you necessarily want to hang around with," he replied. "And then there's the armed security guards."

"What are they keeping inside? Fort Knox?"

"Maybe." Daniel frowned. "I'm serious. These guys mean business."

"Good to know." Harley nodded. "I'll see what I come up with then."

At that, Harley slapped his buddy on the shoulder. "I'll

see you in a couple hours." And he headed out.

JASMINE WILLOUGHBY SAT out on the deck, brushing the strands of hair off her face. It was a hot evening, and the iced lemonade wasn't making a dent in her frustration or her sadness. Her son, Jimmy, had gone over to his friend's house. She could hear them in the backyard on the trampoline. They were just two houses down and being as obnoxiously loud as eleven-year-old boys could be.

Her mother was inside the house, weeping softly into her hanky, as she was wont to do daily. To know that the only way out of this life was her mother's death was not something Jasmine wanted to contemplate, but, on back-to-back sad days, it was hard not to. Particularly right now as Jasmine wished she and Jimmy were a long way away from all this.

She groaned, as she sat here, her eyes closed. She tried so hard to make her mother feel at home, but the situation was just getting out of control.

Jasmine may have to look at putting her mom into a seniors' home, and she knew her mother wouldn't deal very well with that. If she slid into full-blown dementia, where she didn't know anybody around her, then maybe that would be okay because her mom wouldn't feel like she'd been abandoned. But she was lucid just enough times and just for long enough minutes that it wouldn't work out. Her mother would feel completely lost.

As it was, her mom remembered all the bad things and none of the good things. How did that happen? Why would she be stuck in a time loop where she only remembered the things that she was upset at her daughter about? And there been plenty of those. Jasmine had had a wild streak, and she'd run hard and fast in the wrong direction way back then, particularly after Harley left.

She'd been heartbroken, devastated even, and had gone more than a little crazy for a while there. Finding out she was pregnant had calmed things down in her mind, but it just raised all kinds of hell with her parents. Particularly when she didn't tell them until she was already well past her first trimester. She was close to twenty-three weeks when her mother made a comment about Jasmine getting fat, and she'd snapped back that she wasn't fat, that she was pregnant. That had caused the storm of all storms. Not that she was particularly proud of her behavior at that moment, sharing the news, but her child didn't have to pay the price.

As it was, her father had died not long afterward, and her mother had needed Jasmine in a big way but was already showing signs. But, if not for that series of events, Jasmine didn't quite know where she would have ended up. Because she knew her parents were ready to turn her out of the house and had had consistent arguments about it. Jasmine was sure that her mother was in favor of kicking her out.

At the time it seemed more like her father didn't want to toss her out but was more about looking for a husband for her. Something she just didn't understand, but it came back down to her father's belief that a female needed to have a man to look after them. But then this was all ground zero, and there was just no answer that would make it any better.

As she sat here, a huge black truck drove down the street and slowed in front of her house. She frowned, as she looked at the driver. Something was just so familiar about him. She hopped to her feet, trying to get closer, but she didn't recognize the truck.

The driver turned the truck around, came back, parked on the opposite side of the road, and stared directly at her. She shook her head, not sure what she saw, but she walked over to the front steps, leaned against the pillar on the porch, and sipped her lemonade. When the man hopped out of the truck, slammed the door closed, and walked toward her with a rapid but slightly uneven stride, she still didn't recognize him.

When he approached the sidewalk, he looked up at her. "Hello, Jasmine."

She stopped and stared, and then her heart slammed against her chest. "What the hell are you doing here?"

He gave a small half smile. "Well, it wasn't for you apparently. I came back to do a job."

"I knew you would never come back, no matter what you tried to tell me back then." Her back stiffened, as she leveled a glare at the only man she'd ever loved.

"Maybe," he said quietly. "But you also knew that, being only sixteen, there was no way I could stay with you until you were an adult."

"Yeah? And what happened when I hit that age?"

"Doesn't matter. You found somebody else, either before I left or soon afterward," he noted in a hard voice. "As rumors say, you have a child."

"I do." Her tone was defiant, having heard so much all her life about her single-motherhood status—and most of it unpleasant—she immediately glared at him. "And it's none of your damn business."

He slowly nodded. "Well, that's true because I know it's not mine. Did you tell everybody it was though?"

She shrugged. "I knew you weren't coming back, so it

didn't matter what I said."

"I made a good scapegoat, right? Everybody was more than willing to believe that's who I was." He shook his head, as if disappointed in her.

At that, she felt a twinge of remorse. "Honestly I wasn't thinking very clearly at the time at all. I was only sixteen, as you remember, and about to have a baby."

"And that's my fault? Because that's not fair."

She hesitated and then slowly shook her head. "No, you're right. It wasn't your fault. I would have been happier if it had been your child."

"Wouldn't have happened. I told you that I made a promise to your parents."

"Well, guess what? They didn't believe me when I told them that the baby wasn't yours."

"Did you tell them?"

"I did, but my dad was already in a rampage, thinking it was yours, and I couldn't dissuade him from that."

"Did you try?"

He widened his stance, a little on the aggressive side for her liking. But she could kind of see his point. "I did. But he and I were already at loggerheads for him sending you away, and I wasn't very happy when I found out I was pregnant anyway. And I didn't tell them until you were long gone and until I was so many months down that pathway that they couldn't force me to terminate the pregnancy."

"Did you ever tell him who the father was?"

"No, my father died shortly after Jimmy was born."

"I'm sorry about that." Harley frowned.

"Dad was basically a good man, but he was hard." She sighed, relaxing against the post. "But then you know that."

"And I tried hard to play by his rules." He walked up the

steps toward her.

"You did, dammit." She laughed. But she took a long sip of her lemonade. "You haven't changed much."

"I've changed a lot."

"So I wonder, if now, present day, would you have left me behind?"

"Because I made that promise? Yes. My word means everything."

"To even the woman you love?"

"You were a child and underage, and I needed to get away."

She stared at him, her gaze thirstily on his face, as she studied the man she'd waited for, hoping against hope that he would someday return. "I didn't sleep at night," she said quietly, "hoping that I would hear you coming back."

"I went into the navy." His tone was harsh. "Coming back would only be when I was on leave. And apparently you were already pregnant with another man's child, when I was on my first leave."

"Did you come back here then?"

"No. I didn't get leave. I ended up doing extra work on base because we had a riot happening," he admitted. "That seemed to set the pattern for the next few years. I got very little time off. I was supposed to, and I banked it, but every time I thought about coming back here, I figured you'd moved on. And, of course, I was right."

She stared at him flatly. "When I realized that you had *rejected* me, I went out to a big party, got drunk, and I don't remember what happened," she explained. "I somehow got home. Woke up the next morning, and my clothes were a bloody mess, and my body was bruised. I felt fine but sore, and I found out I was pregnant a few months later."

He stopped and stared. "Seriously?"

She nodded mutely. "And there was not one damn person I could tell who would listen. I don't know who my son's father is. But whoever it is, as far as I'm concerned, raped me that night."

"Were you drugged?"

"I didn't get tested," she murmured. "I tried telling the sheriff. Nobody believed me. I hid in shame, until I couldn't hide it from parents any longer."

He stopped, closed his eyes, and swore.

She nodded. "I did plenty of that too. And then I figured that, even if you did come back, you'd take one look at me, and you'd run away."

"Not because of that. Daniel just told me that I had a child. It was a bit of a shock. Because, of course, I knew I didn't have one."

She nodded slowly. "And I wouldn't have passed it off as yours, except that nobody would believe me. Everybody insisted that you were the father, no matter what I said."

"Of course. I made a great scapegoat. Did you ever tell your parents what really happened?"

"No," she admitted slowly. "At the beginning, I was just too upset and confused. Figured that I deserved whatever had happened because I went to the party and because I was drinking. As you well know, I couldn't handle alcohol very easily. Still can't."

"No. You never did do very well with that, and you were so young that it made sense."

"Well, it doesn't matter because I certainly drank as a way to try to forget that you had left me." She shrugged. "I went wild once you were gone."

"To be expected. A little bit of rebellion never hurt anybody."

"Until she wakes up the next day, not remembering anything, with a massive headache, and finding out a few months later that she's pregnant." Her voice was harsh. "And you want to talk about feeling alone? Yeah, that was me then."

"And, of course, your parents would never have accepted my child either."

"But neither could they afford to send me away, which was their alternative answer for their shame."

"I'm sure they relied on the church to make their decisions. and I'm sorry for whatever happened to you."

She lifted her gaze above him and shrugged. "So am I in many ways, … but, once I realized I would be a mom, I still hoped for the longest time that you'd come back here, and then I gave up hope, and I started living again. But I didn't get a chance to live much, what with my father's sudden death. In that way, my mother became very dependent on me and very quickly ended up with Alzheimer's, and I still don't know if it was all related."

"If it's possible, I'm sure it was. Your parents were very interdependent."

"That's a good way to put it." She laughed, then looked at him. "And why are you here now?"

CHAPTER 2

MAYBE JASMINE SHOULDN'T have been so harsh in her original greeting, but it had been a shock. All she could think about were the nights that she'd laid here, hoping and hoping and hoping that Harley would actually return, and yet knowing in her heart of hearts that he had never planned to. That he just said that to keep her quiet and happy. She sighed. "Did you ever even *think* about coming back?"

"All the time." Steadily he looked at her, then smiled. "I really cared. You know that."

"And yet you didn't come back, ... so how much did you really care?"

"I cared enough to leave you to make decisions on your own and to see what you really wanted for your life. Did you ever get flowers on your birthday those first three years after I left?"

She frowned. "Flowers were delivered here. I remember being surprised. But it's not like I knew they were mine, other than it was on my birthday."

"Well, that was me."

She stared at him, frowning. "Seriously?"

"Yeah, for some reason, I thought you'd figure that out."

"How was I supposed to figure that out?" She shook her head. "Nobody could figure that out. No word from you in almost a year, and, all of a sudden, flowers arrive out of the blue. My name wasn't on them."

"I didn't want to make it too obvious, and I didn't want, … in case you had found a partner or married or done something, … I didn't want to cause trouble. But I figured when you saw that they were daffodils that you would know."

She stared at him and sagged against the steps. "Oh my God. I never made that association."

"That it was daffodils?" He looked at her in surprise.

The corner of her lips kicked up. "That the daffodils were from you and were sent to me. I thought at the time it was a very strange choice for flowers because most people didn't deliver daffodils. It was always roses or other types of floral bouquets."

"But at the time that we were together," he explained cautiously, "daffodils were your favorite."

"That's quite true." She smiled. "They still are."

"And you didn't once wonder?"

She looked at him immediately and slowly shook her head.

"Wow." He shoved his hands in his pockets. "That's something I didn't expect."

"I guess we were both a little on the dense side back then." She finally burst into a laugh. "I just can't imagine. Here I'd be, sitting, staring at these flowers, and you're probably waiting for somebody to contact you."

"Well, a card was there too. Did you get that?"

She frowned and nodded. "Sure, nothing but a bunch of numbers, not my name."

"Yes. My phone number."

"I didn't even dial it. It wasn't written like a, … like a

phone number." She frowned. "I don't even remember if I still have it. I'm pretty sure I don't. I know my mother was pretty upset that I could be getting flowers."

"Why?" he asked in an odd tone.

She smiled. "Because she was sure that they were hers and that they were from my father. Mind you, this was after his death. And was my first real indication that she was losing her memory. As I recall at the time, I didn't have any reason to believe they were for me. I just told her that they were for her to make her happy."

"Wow." He stared at her, shook his head. "That's just bizarre."

"The whole thing's bizarre," she admitted. "Including the fact that you sent me daffodils and didn't leave a note."

"I did leave a note. I left you my phone number."

"I'm not sure that came through. It wasn't … It was missing a digit, I think. It wasn't the ten digits. It was like nine, … nine digits. Not ten."

He frowned and then he started to laugh. "You know what? Something so simple, like that, would sink a ship because it's just a stupid error."

"Well, you had to phone in the order, I presume?"

"Yes, I phoned it in and asked to have it delivered on your birthday," he murmured.

"Well, they did get that right." She smirked. "But not a whole lot else."

"Damn," he muttered again. "Where's your son now?"

"Over at his friend's." She had answered absentmindedly. Now she studied him more intently. "And why are you in town? You never did answer me."

He motioned at the steps. "May I sit?"

Immediately she backed up, so there was room for two.

"Go ahead."

He sat down and explained about the War Dog.

"So you got your dream to join the navy."

"I really did. And then I got badly injured in an accident, and I'm now no longer in the navy."

She froze. "Oh, my God, are you hurt?"

"Well, I'm not the same, not as whole as I was before, but I'm okay."

"But not capable of doing your job in the navy?" she asked curiously.

"Not the kind of job I was doing, and I didn't want the kind of job I was capable of doing at the time. So I discharged out."

"And now what?"

"Well, I haven't been out of rehab very long. I was helping this one group in New Mexico, and then this job came up to find the dog, for which I was more than happy to get out of town for a bit."

"Why?"

"I just needed a break. Doing lots of thinking about my life and what I want to do with it and how different it is to be here compared to where I thought I'd be at this point."

"Did you ever get married, have kids?"

"Nope, I didn't." He paused, then chuckled. "I understand Daniel has two boys and a third child on the way through." A big grin filled his face.

She laughed. "Yes, I see him every once in a while. I see his wife more often than not."

"I couldn't believe it when he told me who he'd married." Harley shook his head. "She was always the head of the class."

"She still is. He probably didn't tell you that she is a

doctor." Harley stared at her in shock. "After medical school she came home, and that's when the two of them got together."

"Wow. Well, good for both of them. And you?" he asked. "Did you ever get married, have any other children?"

She looked at him in surprise. "Are you kidding? I'm the infamous one with a bad rep in town. I got a ton of invitations, but you can bet they weren't the kind I wanted to accept. Never been to a party since."

"I'm sorry. That's really shitty."

"Not only shitty but, after my father died and my mother became sick, it was, … then I became a single parent to two kids. It's like your entire adult life is defined by all those events." She sighed the sigh of a worn-out parent. "I couldn't go out with friends. I didn't have babysitters because somebody had to look after not only Mom but my son." She shook her head. "This has been my life. Very quiet and boring."

"And I'm sorry for that too. You were hoping to travel and to see the world."

"Yeah, that died a quick death with my pregnancy."

HARLEY WAS HAPPY that at least there was no bitterness against her son in her voice. "Do you have any idea who it is who did this to you?"

She shook her head. "A lot of people were at the party, when I got there." She shrugged. "It could have been anyone."

"Anybody else end up pregnant after that?"

She looked at him in surprise. "I didn't even think of

that. I don't know. I didn't have a whole lot of girlfriends back then, what with my parents keeping me fairly isolated—allowing only the people who they thought were *worthy*."

"And that's a challenge, isn't it?" he murmured. "Because you always felt like you had nobody."

"Of course I felt like that. They didn't let me have sleepovers. They didn't let me go on trips with anybody else—only the church-approved ones that they allowed me to go on. And then, when I did go someplace, it was on my own, mostly out of rebellion and hurt because you'd left me," she explained. "And I ended up pregnant."

"And for that alone your father would have been incredibly angry."

"I don't know if he was angry so much as disappointed. It was very difficult to tell him. As it was, I held off telling them anything, and then more or less threw it in their faces when we were having an argument."

"Even to have argued with them, that's something you would never have done before."

"I changed a lot over that. I pretty well knew what had happened immediately when I woke up the next morning, but again I was ashamed and didn't know who to turn to, didn't have a support system, and sure as heck wouldn't go to the hospital or the authorities on my own before all that. Even afterward, facing it alone, I didn't figure the authorities would even listen to me, and when I told them, and they proved to me that they weren't listening …" She shook her head for a long moment. "So I just hid it all and became a bit of a recluse. It wasn't an easy time."

"No, of course not," Harley was thinking about all Jasmine had been through in such a short time frame. "To lose me, to find out you're pregnant, to lose your father, and then to have your mother in this deteriorating condition, hats off to you for even keeping your sanity."

"Did I say I was sane?" she asked calmly.

He chuckled. "You still have the same dry wit."

"Other than my son, it's about all I have." She gave a heavy sigh. She looked at him. "We're a hell of a pair."

"Well, it's a case of life gives us something that we weren't expecting. And it's up to us to try to make the most of it."

"Yeah, I don't feel very philosophical these days."

"Did you ever do any secondary education, training, anything?"

"Nope, I just had courses in real life," she replied, with a touch of bitterness.

"Understood. Just the death of your father would have been tough."

"And I had to deal with Mother after that. Since then, it's been dealing with medical bills, trying to keep the bills paid, wondering why my father hadn't set things up better, and all that good stuff."

"I thought you guys were well off?"

"No, apparently they took in foster kids, like you, to pay the bills." He stopped and stared. She nodded. "I know. It wasn't exactly the high and mighty role that Dad proclaimed he was doing it for."

"Interesting. He had a good job. He was an accountant."

"Yes, but for a small company that couldn't afford to pay him more, and apparently my father didn't do well with change so didn't want to change companies."

"I'm sorry." He frowned. "Did you ever get any other foster kids after I left?"

"No, and it was one of the things that my dad was kind of bitter about because he figured that, at least if I were a foster kid, or they had taken in my son as a foster, as they did take him in obviously," she noted, "Dad would have got paid for him."

"Ouch," Harley murmured.

"Yes, apparently that was a big thing for him."

"And then did you have any medical attention during your pregnancy?"

"Not much." She shrugged. "Only the absolute minimum."

"Sounds like you've had a tough time, no matter which way you look at it."

She smiled. "But you made it though."

"A little older, more battered, injured, but recovering." He shifted his hand and rotated it so she could see. As her eye widened he nodded, looked at his truck. "I should go. I'll take a trip north and see where this dog is."

"It's a pretty rough area up there," she warned.

"So Daniel tells me." He smiled, turned to face her. "You're looking good." And he stood and walked toward his truck.

"Is that it?" she called after him.

He turned. "What else would you like me to say?"

"I don't know. How about a coffee out?" she asked.

He looked at her with interest. "You got a babysitter?"

She snorted. "If anybody told Jimmy that he needed a babysitter at eleven, that would be a completely interesting scene. As for my mother, well …" Jasmine looked back at the house and then nodded. "You're right. I probably can't leave her."

"Well then, why don't I go pick up coffee on my way

back?" he suggested.

She hesitated.

He added, "Or not. But, if you can't leave the house, that doesn't leave us much choice."

"No, it doesn't."

Just then the front door opened, and a frail lady stepped out on the porch. Harley recognized her. Matilda was nothing if not always very prim and proper, but this was definitely a much more messed-up version. "Hello, Matilda," he called out gently, as he walked closer.

She turned and looked at him, her eyes opened wide, and she screamed. "You," she snapped. "How dare you?"

He looked at her in surprise. "How dare I what?" He looked from Matilda back to Jasmine in confusion.

"You're supposed to mow the lawn and didn't!" she screeched.

He looked at her with even more surprise, back at Jasmine. "Wow."

"I told you." She reached out on arm for her mother, but her mother was having nothing to do with it.

"How dare you let him on this property," she snapped, staring at Jasmine. "I told you last time no way he was allowed to be here."

"It's not the lawn-mowing guy, Mom."

Her mother looked at her in shock and again at him. "Of course it is." But a little bit of doubt was in her voice.

"No. No, it isn't. This is Harley."

"Harley." She frowned.

Jasmine nodded. "Yes, Harley. Remember? You had him as a foster son for many years."

"No, that boy was nothing but trouble. We had to be really on his case to keep him out of trouble all the time.

That was a very hard-earned paycheck."

At that, Jasmine looked at Harley and whispered, "I'm sorry."

Harley snorted. "Oh, I know. It wasn't easy being here as part of the household from my side either."

"Hey, you at least got to leave."

He winced at that. "That's a very good point." He looked at Matilda, who, just as if a switch had turned on, pivoted to him and smiled.

"Hi. How are you? What's your name?" And she reached out a hand to shake his, even though she was at the top of the steps, and he was at the bottom. "My name is Matilda."

"Hi, Matilda. My name is Harley."

"Ah. I used to have a son, … a foster son, you know. That was his name too."

"Yes, that's me. I was your foster son."

She smiled. "Nice to meet you. It's a beautiful day, isn't it?" Then she looked at the glass in Jasmine's hand. "Oh my, did you make lemonade?" Jasmine held out her glass. Her mother took a sip and spat it out and immediately turned into another personality. "Oh, this is terrible, absolutely terrible. I'll make some good stuff." She waved at the two of them. "Now you just wait here, and I'll go get my famous lemonade." And she disappeared inside.

Harley stared at the door. "How long will that conversation remain in her head?"

"Five minutes maximum, maybe even only five seconds," she said, fatigued. "Sometimes she's better than others."

"Like all of us, I imagine. … She is quite a challenge for you, isn't she?"

"She is, indeed. I've been wondering if I need to look at

putting her in a home, but it's hard for me to do that. Plus, I'm not sure I can afford it."

"She's still healthy though, physically?"

"Yes. So the only reason to put her in a home is if I can't look after her."

"And, of course, that's a very difficult decision to make, isn't it?"

Just then a crash came inside the house. Jasmine looked at Harley in shock and bolted indoors. He raced up the steps behind her, and they found Matilda on the kitchen floor, shattered glass from a pitcher still in her hand, water everywhere. She lay here dazed, staring up at the ceiling.

"Don't move, Mom. Don't move," Jasmine ordered. "Let me get some of this glass away from you."

But the older lady struggled to put her hands down and to get up and seemed to be completely unaware that she sat amid shattered glass.

Harley stepped in, picked her up under her arms, and lifted her ever-so-gently out of all the glass, while Jasmine grabbed a broom and tried to clean up the mess. Matilda looked at him and burst into tears and collapsed into his arms. He looked over at Jasmine.

She nodded. "Can you take her into the living room and sit her down in the big chair?" she asked softly. "I'll clean up this mess."

CHAPTER 3

JASMINE QUICKLY CLEANED up the glass but was a little confused because there was so much of it. Her gaze went around the windows, and then she called out urgently, "Harley, come here. Quick."

He immediately popped around the doorway. "What's the matter?" And she pointed. He stared and frowned. "Good Lord." He stepped carefully around the glass on the floor and took a look at a piece of glass still in a pane in the window frame.

"That's a bullet hole, isn't it?" she whispered.

He nodded, his face grim, as he stared silently around the backyard. "Have you been shot at before?"

She snorted. "What kind of question is that?" she asked. "Of course not."

He turned to look at her. "So what's changed?"

She shrugged and shook her head. "Nothing. Nothing's changed. Nothing here ever changes. It's the same damn town. It's the same damn life that I was living before. Nothing's changed."

But his gaze wouldn't let her off the hook.

She raised her eyebrow, still shaking her head. "The only thing that's different is that you walked into my life."

Immediately his brows drew together, with a harsh peak in the center. "And why would that cause something like this?" He waved his hand to the window.

"I don't know. I really don't know." She asked, "Is there any chance he's still around?"

"Of course there's a chance, but it was your mother here in the kitchen at the time."

"Yes." And then she took a slow deep breath. "But we also have the same blond hair. And we're both the same height. And I don't know if somebody would have recognized that it was her or me in the kitchen. Depends on how far away they were."

"So you're thinking that bullet might have been for you?" Immediately his gaze went to the opposite wall.

"Or it was a warning. I don't know." She started to shiver. "I don't know what to say."

He immediately walked over, pulled her into his arms, and just held her close. "It's okay. You're safe."

"Thank God that Jimmy wasn't here. And I'm safe at the moment, but that was a bullet."

"And not likely a stray bullet either, not given how it came through into the kitchen." As he stood here, he saw a direct line of sight to the street on the far side of the property fence line. "Have you had any problems with anybody in town?"

"No." She frowned. "Remember? This is just some small town outside of Eureka. A town where nothing happens. I got pregnant, and that has been the most exciting thing for people to talk about for more than a decade now." Enough bitterness was in her voice that she knew she hadn't quite dealt with it. She stepped back. "Let me finish cleaning up the glass. I don't want my mother coming back in here just yet."

"She's sitting in her recliner and not moving."

"She gets like that sometimes. Right now it's a blessing." She quickly scooped up the rest of the glass, casting one more glance over at the bullet hole in the window and shook her head. "I don't even know what to do now."

"Well, we need to clean the glass off the counter. If you've got some plywood around here, I can nail it up to seal off that window—until you can get the pane replaced. And I suggest you call the sheriff."

She looked up at him in surprise and then nodded. "I guess that's the most sensible thing, isn't it?"

"When people start shooting, then that's generally what the most practical response is, yes."

She quickly cleaned up the countertop, as he lifted items off the counter, and then wiped it into the garbage can. Afterward, she took a wet paper towel and wiped down the counter again, looking for little bits of shards. And finally, with that all cleaned up, she walked into the living room, Harley following her.

There was Mom, still sitting in the chair where Harley had placed her. "Mom, are you okay?"

Her mother looked up at her, smiled. "Hi, how are you?"

Her heart sank. "I'm fine, Mom. How are you?"

"I'm just fine, dear." She patted the seat beside her. "Just sit down and relax. You work so hard."

"Yes, I do." She sagged into the chair. She stared with deep sadness at her mother. "Do you know who I am?"

"Yes. You're the lady who cleans up for me. I do appreciate the hard work you put into it."

"I'm not the cleaning lady, Mom. … I'm Jasmine, your daughter."

"No, no, no. My daughter died many years ago, in

childbirth."

As that was the first time she'd ever said something like that, Jasmine felt her jaw drop. She looked over at Harley.

"Any chance that's how she felt about it?"

She stared at him, looked back at her mother, her own heart starting to break. "It's quite likely, yes. … They were very much about appearances. Doing the right thing but not necessarily for the right reason."

She stared at her mom, feeling tears in the back of her throat. Had her mother always felt like that? Was the truth just coming out now that there were no filters? But then, at the same time, there was also no logical sense to make of the way her mother's brain was working right now either.

"If she doesn't know who you are, it might be easier to reconsider a home."

"Every day." She nodded. "Every damn day. I want to help her. I'm just not sure that I'm capable of doing it the way it needs to be done."

"And, if she doesn't recognize who you are," he noted quietly, "she won't notice if she's in a home."

"But I will. I was raised to be a dutiful daughter."

"*Duty* isn't the same as *love*."

"No, it isn't," she agreed, "and I'm not sure I have the money for her to go into a home."

"Did they not have enough for themselves to look after them in old age?"

"Those homes are expensive." She shrugged. "I'll have to look into her health care plan and at the options. I've been meaning to do it for months, and I keep putting it off. She'll have several bad days, and I start in that direction. Then she has a good day, and I stop."

"You need to be easier on yourself too. Not everybody is

capable of looking after their mother when they get in this condition."

"I just don't see her improving," she added sadly. "She could be like this for another thirty years or more. She's only turning sixty this year. If she fits the guidelines, she might get more government assistance."

"And alternatively, which is where your concern is, she could be thirty more years in a home, if there's money to pay for it."

"Yes. Although maybe I have to sell the house first. I just don't know. It's like a life sentence in some ways."

"You love her."

"But this isn't the woman I know."

"Not to mention this one isn't exactly a woman you have been terribly close to."

Her mother's future was something that deeply troubled Jasmine. Her father had passed on early, and her mother had declined very quickly after that, but then she hit a plateau, where she seemed to live in her own world. Nice for her but not so nice for everybody around her. At least she was still fully functioning healthwise, so there wasn't any home care required.

Not yet.

But, other than that, her mother had to have a babysitter all the time, which Jasmine was, and since she had an eleven-year-old, that was fine. She would be housebound anyway. She wasn't sure what she would do when Jimmy hit sixteen or eighteen though because that would be a whole new change for all of them. She didn't want to see her entire life at home being solely looking after her mother.

As it was, Jasmine felt like she'd missed a turn in the road somewhere along the line, and she didn't have anybody to blame but herself. But, when she was really at her lowest point, it was easy to turn against Harley. She reached out a hand to her mom. "Are you feeling okay, Mom?" Her gaze searched her mother's face, looking for any sign that glass had hit her.

Her mother looked back at her with a bright smile and a completely vacant look. "I'm fine, dear."

Jasmine nodded. "In that case, I think I'll go make a cup of tea." She stumbled to the kitchen, choking back a cry of pain.

Harley stood at the front door, watching her retreat in the opposite direction. "I'll go outside and take a look around."

"You do that." She waved her hand dismissively at him.

He hesitated.

She glared. "Go. That's what you do best. Just go." She was immediately sorry for snapping because his gaze narrowed, as if to say something, then nodded, turned, and walked out. She watched him go—resentment, anger, and regret in her heart.

WELL, JASMINE HAD certainly left Harley with no doubt about how she felt, although she was under a lot of stress with her mother. Whatever the hell had just happened here with the damn bullet added to it. And that's the part that pissed him right off. Somebody had shot into her kitchen. She had had a child eleven years ago and had been looking after her mother and son ever since. Her life was not the way she had wanted it to go; it's not the way she had planned it, and nothing ever exciting happened. This is just what it was.

And he could tell that she wanted to change it, to get out, to live differently, to make it more exciting, but more exciting didn't mean getting shot at. It was also telling when she had mentioned that the only difference was that Harley had arrived in her world today.

What possible reason could there be for somebody—if somebody had known that Harley was here and had actually known that he was here at this house—to have shot her? He'd made more than a few enemies on missions, but they'd had plenty of time in the last couple years to locate him and to take him out while he was an invalid. It didn't make any sense to try something like this while he was now on his feet and in better health than he had been in years.

Jasmine hadn't yet made any comment about his arm, but then he had a glove on it too. He stared down at the prosthetic. At least it was his left side; he could still do an awful lot with his right. He also had on a jacket, so she probably hadn't seen much. And that would explain a lot too.

He slipped outside and moved to the far side of the house and up alongside the wooden fence. The fence was only four feet tall. He was pretty sure that the line of sight had been direct and clear from that back corner. As he walked to the area where he thought the shooter could have been standing, he confirmed no sign of an intruder's footprints inside the fence, but, at only four feet tall, it would have been easy hop.

He made the jump himself without too much effort, and, as he landed, he stopped and looked around. This was a corner lot, and so there was traffic on both sides, and the shooter could easily have pulled up, walked to the fence, made the shot, got back in the car, and left. It was also possible that a passerby could have just done it. It was not a very long distance, so a handgun might have taken care of it too.

He frowned at that because, if so, no great skill had been required then. He walked the fence along the backside but returned where his earlier assessment was. No footprints. A gravel path ran along the road. Anybody could have stopped and not been seen because of even a short wooden fence. He turned to look around. It was a wide street. Even if security cameras were on a neighboring house on the far side, this happened at the back of Jasmine's house, and chances were any security cams wouldn't register anything this far over. He hadn't checked but assumed that no security cameras were here on Jasmine's home, and, if there were any street cams, they wouldn't be this far out from the main avenues.

In other words, somebody had managed to come in, taken a shot, and left without being seen. With that, he hopped the fence again, walked the entire perimeter, came back to the front of the house, looking for street cameras, but there were none. It was a small town, and this area was a small set of blocks back off the main street. He walked back inside the front of the house to see Jasmine sitting in the kitchen, huddling over a cup of tea. Matilda was sitting in the same chair with the same placid look on her face, a cup of tea cooling at her side.

Harley walked through to the kitchen and heard a bit of sniffling. His heart ached for the situation Jasmine was in. He pulled up a chair, sat down, and, not giving her a chance to argue, quickly picked up one of her hands in his. "I think you need to find another solution."

"Any solution I find racks me over with guilt."

"I know. Change is hard. Letting go is hard, even in bad

relationships. You just have to look after yourself and your son. When is he due back?"

"I'm not sure," she murmured and looked up at the kitchen clock nearby. "Probably in the next twenty minutes or so."

He nodded. "It's almost dark out. The shooter chose a good time."

"Meaning that he'd be hidden or that we'd be in the kitchen?"

"It's possible he was there for a while, waiting for somebody to go into the kitchen."

She looked over at him. "Where are you staying?"

"I have a room above the pub."

She snorted at that. "Wow, that's just like old times."

"It is in many ways, yes. I'd like to meet Daniel's family, but other than that I don't want to interfere in his life too much."

"When you walked, you walked away from all of us, didn't you?"

"Yes, I did. It was easier on me to have a clean break."

"And I guess we're always supposed to do what's easier on us, huh?"

"No, I don't think so. I think it's a case of trying to do what you need to do to survive. I had to leave here. Otherwise you would end up pregnant with my baby," he declared bluntly.

She looked up at him and gave a quick nod. "Well, that was the hope at least."

"I couldn't look after you. I couldn't afford to keep you, much less a baby. and I'd already made a promise to your father—and to myself—which I had no intention of breaking."

"You never really liked living here, did you?"

"With you, yes. You were the light of my life," he murmured, squeezing her fingers. "Your parents, not so much. I was here because they were getting a paycheck. Other than that I knew perfectly well I'd be on the street. I was smart enough to toe the line to finish high school and to get into the navy, but I didn't forget you. Never you."

"Oh, you forgot," she stated. "Every time you got busy doing something fun, you forgot about me. I didn't have those distractions."

He bowed his head. "Maybe. Temporarily yes. As life has a habit of doing, things interfered. Yes, I had other relationships, but I certainly didn't have anything that matched the same care and affection that we had."

"So why didn't you come back?"

"Because so much time had passed that I figured you'd moved on, and, to be honest, I didn't want confirmation of that. It was a blow when I found out from Daniel that you'd had *my* child."

"Yeah, after the initial confrontations, I didn't even bother trying to explain myself."

He nodded. "It was quite a shock. Because, of course, the only two people who would know that it's not my son are you and me. Believe me. A part of me wishes he was."

She looked at him in surprise and then shook her head. "What crazy webs we weave," she murmured. "Back then I was so young that I had no clue what having a child would mean. I would have seduced you, if I thought I could have. But you kept turning me away."

"Because of the promises I made. You were also very young. You didn't have your parents' permission to wed, even though I talked to your father about it."

She stared at him, shocked. "You did?"

I did," he admitted. "Even though we were young, and it probably wasn't the best idea, he was very adamant about the fact that absolutely no way in hell he'd accept me as a son-in-law. And I knew I needed to leave. Because he wasn't just talking about then, he was talking also in the future."

"Wow," she murmured. "I guess rejection is still a big part of your life too, isn't it?"

"Always has been. It's one of those little bits and pieces of your personality that you have to watch out for when you get into situations. But the navy accepted me. And that acceptance was complete and total. I went into it, knowing that who I was would work out. And I dove into it full force and made a very good life for myself. … But believe me, that rejection is something that always sits with you."

"But I didn't reject you."

"No, you didn't," he agreed. "At the same time, you were also very young, and I couldn't count on you feeling the same in a couple years, particularly if I didn't have a job and you were with a child at your young age."

"I didn't want to stay here, even before you left. You have no idea how hard it was to remain here, even under these circumstances."

"Honestly, I can easily imagine that they made your life hell."

She snorted. "Yeah, that's … that's a good word for it. You can bet that they made me pay in so many ways for my infraction."

"And, of course, your father would see it that way, so it was better for him to believe his daughter was a wayward loose woman," he noted sarcastically, "than an innocent victim of likely a date-rape drug."

"Yes, I think so. Because there was shame in both, but, with the one, he could insulate and blame you, and the other one he couldn't."

"And, of course, I made a great scapegoat." Harley nodded. "Always did. Everything that went wrong in his life was because of me."

"He really did that, didn't he?" she said, marveling. "I forgot. Even at dinnertime, if he'd had a shitty day, it would have all been because of something that you did that set him off first thing in the morning."

"I remember. I spent a lifetime trying to avoid him. But my options were another foster home or leave on my own, when I wasn't quite old enough to take care of business." He shook his head. "Even now I often consider that, thinking that I should have just left. Any other foster home would have been better."

"But it might not have been, … at least we were the devil you know."

"It had nothing to do with the devil," he stated quietly. "It had everything to do with the angel that you were."

She looked at him in surprise and then gave him a gentle smile. "Now that's really nice to hear. I didn't realize you were staying for my sake."

"For at least the last two to three years here. Before that, I really wasn't old enough to make much in the way of decisions at all."

"He did talk about getting rid of you at one time too," she murmured.

Harley nodded. "He told me that. Told me that I was only here short-term, and, if I crossed that line one more time, I was done." He smiled. "I didn't realize they needed that paycheck. That makes more sense than anything."

"If that makes sense, well, I guess we can park that for now." She rubbed her face, looked up at the clock again. "Jimmy should be home any minute." She withdrew her hand from his.

"Do you want me to leave?"

She shrugged. "It doesn't matter," she said. "I'll only introduce you as my foster brother anyway."

"Well, you could, or you could just say I'm an old friend." At that, the front door opened and a tall, skinny streak of a youth stormed into the kitchen. "Mom, I need a snack before bed."

She snorted. "Of course you do." She smiled. "You're never full."

"Hey, I'm growing up. Have to be big and strong." At that, he stopped and stared. "Oh, I didn't know you had company."

"This is Harley"—she pointed—"and he spent much of his childhood years here with Grandma and Grandpa."

"Oh, he was the foster kid." Jimmy reached out a hand. "I'm Jimmy. I can't imagine you were here the whole time."

"Actually I was taken away twice. More as a warning."

At that, Jasmine looked at him sharply. "You were?"

"I was. It was your father's way of keeping me in control."

She winced. "Yeah, Grandpa wasn't the nicest of people."

"See? And he died long enough ago that I don't even know him," Jimmy said. "But I haven't heard a whole lot of nice things."

"Everybody's got a nice side, but everybody has that ugly side too," Harley explained.

"Right." He looked back at his mom. "Food?" he asked

hopefully.

"There's still some leftover spaghetti in the fridge."

"Oh, right." He immediately dug into the fridge and pulled out various covered dishes, and, while they watched, he mixed up noodles and sauce and put it in the microwave.

"Feeding him is a never-ending job."

"I think that goes for all kids." Harley nodded.

"As I recall, my parents weren't generous with food for you," she noted. "Maybe that's why Jimmy's appetite here is a surprise."

"I was always hungry, even when I had a part-time job. One of the reasons I went into fast food was so I could get meals for free."

"Well, it also gave you money."

He looked over at her, smiled with a lip tilt. "Which I paid your father half."

She stopped and gaped at him. "What?"

"Yep. He commandeered half of my wages for room and board because I was eating more and causing them more pain and trouble than he was getting paid for to look after me."

She sat back in shock. "You never told me. I imagined you had all this money when you left."

"I didn't have very much at all. The navy was a really good answer. Believe me. I took it and ran."

"Jesus. I didn't realize how bad my father was."

"Or your mother," he murmured. "She's the one who used to sit here on payday, with her hand out."

She was so ashamed of her parents. "She took even more, after my father demanded half? I just …" And then she stopped and shook her head. "No wonder you left. I can't imagine that you stayed as long as you did."

"I needed my high school education because I didn't know what I wanted to do, and I was determined to get at least that much."

"I'll say," Jimmy added, "but I probably would have told them both to *f*-off."

"Jimmy, stop that."

"I know, Mom. You don't like swearing, but, jeez, there's a time and a place. I mean, it's hard to imagine that empty Grandma was that kind of a terror, but, with mean ol' Grandpa to back her up, maybe."

"And that *empty Grandma* is still your grandmother. You will talk about her with respect."

"Sure." Jimmy shrugged, completely uncaring. He popped more of the spaghetti into the microwave to heat it and put away the rest of the leftovers.

At that, Harley stood, looked down at her. "I think that's enough reminiscing for tonight. I'll head back to the pub, and then I'll go look for the dog."

"Right. At least you're not going tonight." He just gave her a quiet smile and didn't say anything. She groaned. "You are, aren't you?"

He took one look at her and then her son, shrugged. "Pub and to bed sounds good too." And, with that, he smiled. "Nice meeting you, Jimmy."

And he turned and walked out.

CHAPTER 4

"WOW, HE'S REALLY nice," Jimmy said. "Can't believe Grandpa and Grandma were that mean to him."

"I can," she replied tiredly. "Anytime I took on babysitting, they demanded half that money too. But it never occurred to me that they were doing that to him. They were already getting paid for him, getting paid money by the government, getting free education for me, free health care for everybody," she noted. "It was just terrible that they did that. I wish I had some money to pay him back."

"Do we have any money?" Jimmy asked.

She looked at him, smiled, and shook her head. "Essentially no. We are living on the little bit of money to look after Grandma. She owns the house, which is paid for, thank goodness, so it's more or less groceries."

"And if Grandma goes?"

"I'll have to find another job—like this."

"And if you sold the house?"

"It will give us a little bit of money, yes. But we'd still have to then pay rent or to find another place to live."

"Right. In other words, money is an issue."

"It's really an issue," she agreed, "and it's one of the reasons why I can't put your grandmother in a home."

"Harold says that his grandparents are in a home. And the government pays for it."

"And I don't know if that's possible or not. I haven't looked into it. It's on my list of things to do."

"Maybe you should. Might be the answer. Then you could get a job and stay here at the house."

"Which kind of sounds like I'm putting her in a home so I can have her house." She frowned. "And that's not who I am."

"I didn't mean it that way. but there's not a whole lot of Grandma left."

Jasmine winced. Because out of the mouth of babes came the truth; just it was a hard truth. "And, as long as we don't look at it that way," she said, "maybe it's easier."

He grabbed his plate of spaghetti and sat beside her and wolfed it down.

She reached over. "Slow down," she cried out gently. "The food isn't disappearing. It'll be there in the next five minutes too."

He grinned. "Sure, but I'm hungry." He stopped, looked down at the food. "I can't believe Grandpa wouldn't have fed him properly."

"He was a big boy too, back then," she murmured. "And I remember him always being hungry."

"And did you help him?"

"Sure I did, but we also didn't keep a ton of food in the house."

"Probably so that nobody could go take it without asking. We always have granola bars and cookies and stuff."

"We didn't have those when I was growing up. … If Mom could make it, then we had it. Otherwise we didn't spend much money."

"So what did they do with all their money?" he asked curiously.

She stared at him and shrugged. "I'm not sure. I don't know how much they had. I know Grandma doesn't have very much at all. She has a little bit from Grandpa's savings, but that's it. And that's what we're all living on. Which is why I don't have money to get you a new bike, when your friends have them, or other stuff that I know you would want."

And she did have to do some research into a seniors' home. But also where did her loyalties lie? Where did her capabilities lie? And what was it that she needed to do for herself?

Jimmy looked at her and around the house, taking it all in. "Wow." He leaned forward. "Who broke the window?"

"We don't know." She didn't want to share with him that a bullet had gone through the window. And, at that thought, she also wondered where the bullet had gone. Had Harley even thought of that? And then she remembered him at the living room wall and realized that, not only had he thought of it, he'd probably also taken the bullet with him. And then what? He hadn't mentioned it to her at all. She pulled out her phone and realized she didn't have his number either. She shook her head and put her cell down again.

"We'll have to get that fixed," her son noted. "He must have forgotten."

"I'll call somebody tomorrow."

"Okay." He finished off his spaghetti, got up, rinsed out his bowl, and put it in the dishwasher. She smiled because he was so darn good with his chores. "I'm off to bed. School's early. Don't forget I have to go out for basketball practice before class."

She nodded. And he headed upstairs.

As soon as he was out of earshot. she phoned the pub and asked for the room that Harley was staying in. She was patched through. And then it rang and rang, but there was no answer. Of course not. He'd gone out after the damn dog. She also wondered if she should call the sheriff. Of course she should, but then her son would find out about the bullet. Yet she knew somebody on the force, somebody who was a good friend of the family. She called Chester at home because she had that kind of relationship with him, where she used to meet him at church events and some of the volunteer programs.

When he answered the call, he said, "I don't usually hear from you at this time of the night."

"That's because I got trouble." She quietly explained what happened.

"Are you serious?"

"Yeah," she replied. "It missed my mom, and I haven't told my son."

"No, of course not. And Harley's back?" he asked.

"He is, indeed," she murmured. "So lots of events changing in my world right now."

"Wow, that must have been a big shock for him."

She stopped for a moment, not sure what he was talking about; then she just shrugged. "I guess."

"How about I run over in the morning, if you don't want your son to know."

"Right, but then I just thought that it might be a problem anyway."

"You know, if it was a bullet, let me come over right now. You can tell your son that I'm stopping in about one of our volunteer activities."

"Which," she said, "there's the bike race this weekend.

Are you helping out?"

"I'll be there bright and early at seven a.m. sharp."

She laughed. "So now you do have a reason to come over."

"I'm on my way." He disconnected the call.

She walked to the bottom of the stairs and called out, "Jimmy?"

A moment later he had poked his head out of his bedroom door. "Yeah?"

"Chester's coming over. He's trying to convince me to help out at the bike thing on Saturday."

"You might as well just give in, Mom."

"Yeah. I'll show him the broken glass too."

"You should have done that earlier." He shook his head.

She just smiled and headed into the living room; her mom still sat here, maybe even was asleep now. Feeling like the worst daughter in the world, she sat down beside her. "Mom?" Her mother jerked awake. "Hey, let's get you up to bed."

"I am tired." Her mom looked at her. "I don't need your help though. I've been looking after myself for a long time now."

"I know that," Jasmine murmured. "Do you think you can go to sleep?"

"Of course," And she got up in a sprightly mood that surprised Jasmine and went up the stairs. She just wasn't sure if it was safe to leave her mom alone. At the top of the stairs, Matilda opened Jimmy's door. Her son called out, "Grandma, don't do that, please."

At that, Jasmine raced up the stairs and led her mother to her bedroom. "This is your room."

"I know that, but who's that nice young man?"

"My son," she said for probably the millionth time in the last couple years.

"You really should have a husband you know. *Tsk, tsk.*"

Jasmine rolled her eyes at that. "Let's get you into your nightclothes."

"Well, I certainly don't need help with that." And her mother immediately stripped down to her buff, threw her nightie over her body, and crawled into bed.

"Mom, we have to brush your teeth, and we need to take your medications."

"I'm not on any medication. I already brushed my teeth," she replied comfortably.

Groaning, Jasmine knew it would be a difficult night when Mom started out like this. "No, that's not true. Your toothbrush is dry. You forgot."

"I didn't forget," she said in a testy voice. "I don't know who you are, but you can just leave now."

At that, Jasmine heard a car door slam outside, and she realized Chester had arrived. Of course he had. Now it would be one of those nights where she couldn't get her mother to cooperate at all. Sighing, Jasmine knew she had to look after some battles and to let go of others. So she turned and walked out. "When you get back up, go brush your teeth."

"I don't need to be told how to look after myself."

"No, of course not."

Downstairs, she opened the front door, still a bit frazzled.

"Oops. Bad timing?"

"No, just my mother."

He winced. "I'm really sorry about that."

"Me too, but I don't seem to be able to do anything

about her condition right now."

"So show me what I'm to look at."

"I didn't tell my son what it was," she said, "just that somebody broke the window. He told me that I should have called you earlier."

"Well, you should have."

"It was within the last two hours, so …"

At that, Chester just nodded, took one look at the nice neat little hole, and whistled. "That's interesting. A high-powered rifle and left almost no shattering."

"Well, you can see the glass cracking on that part. The rest did shatter all over the kitchen, but it didn't destroy the entire pane."

He stood at the bullet area and turned to look back at the house. "But we'll try to find it."

"You may have to ask Harley about that. I don't think he would have left it in the wall, if he knew it was here."

"And what would he do with it?" he asked, looking at her curiously.

"He ended up as a Navy SEAL," she told him. "I researched him over the years, saw that he had received a couple commendations. But he doesn't talk about it."

Chester's eyebrows shot up. "Wow, that would be bad boy gone good."

"He had a pretty tough time here with my parents," she explained, "not terribly abusive, but it wasn't very warm and welcoming either."

"But you were." Chester chuckled.

"And, as I've said before, he's not Jimmy's father."

"So you say."

"Well, Daniel at the pub already told him that he was, which is why he came straight here."

"Of course he did. That would have been a hell of a conversation."

She didn't say anything, knowing that nobody believed her. Absolutely nobody. And it was so damn bad because Harley had left for a hell of a lot of good reasons, and some she hadn't even been aware of. But now it looked like nobody would believe her either, once again, which was why she'd given up trying to tell people back then.

Chester shook his head, still staring at the window. "So what kind of enemies have you made? I would have thought your life was pretty darn simple."

"I don't know about simple," she replied. "It was routine. And boring. And a lot of other things all to do with looking after my mother, which is very challenging."

"It is. I don't think it has to continue that way though."

"I just have to come around to the point where I'm perfectly capable of looking after her that way."

"But she's having some really bad spells these days, isn't she?"

Jasmine thought back and nodded. "There are times where she just sits in one place for hours on end. Some mornings I go talk to her, but it's like she's not even there. I just don't know what to do. I can't forcibly manhandle her to get up, but she just doesn't seem to even register that she has bodily functions."

"And that's when you start looking at a home."

"I know but …" And she let her voice fall away.

"You can't feel guilty all the time. You have to have a life too."

"And that seems very hard to do," she noted. "It just doesn't seem fair."

"Maybe not, maybe not. But, when you think about it,

other things are in life too."

"But she's my mother."

"I know, but you also have a son to look after. Where do your loyalties lie?"

"At the moment," she replied, "I'm holding with both of them."

"For how long though, before you're the one who cracks. And then what? They have nobody."

"I've heard that a time or two as well." She waved at the bullet hole in her partial window. "I don't think there's anything you can even do about this."

"Nope. I'll open a case file but …" Then he shook his head. "You don't have any security, do you?"

"Nope, and," she added, "I've got no motive for what this was."

"I'm wondering if it wasn't just a drive-by shooting. It probably came from the street over there."

"You think he just propped up a gun and shot into … my house?"

"It's a good chance nobody even knew that it would reach the house. And depending on how far away they were, your neighbors wouldn't have heard it either."

She stared at him in shock. "You think it was like a random accident?"

"I don't know what to think. I don't want to minimize the danger, but all you have is a bullet hole in a window. But you think Harley took the bullet?"

"Probably so."

"I'll ask him. We can run ballistics, see if we get a match. Then we'd have somebody to charge."

"Good," she said. "It was my mother who almost got killed."

He shook his head at that. "And yet the two of you do look a lot alike from a distance."

"I know. I was thinking of that too."

"So all I can tell you is to be careful. And, if anything else happens, call me again."

"Will do." She shivered as she walked him to the door.

He looked back at her. "You might want to consider getting a security system."

"There's no money," she argued, "and, if I have to put my mom in a home, there's really no money."

"Got it." He shrugged. "I know there are government-run homes, particularly for those who don't have money."

"And I may have to do that, but I really don't want to."

"We might not want what life gives us, but that still doesn't mean that we don't have to take it. … Don't have to adjust and accept it. … Sometimes you just can't help everybody."

And still thinking hard on the subject, she locked up, feeling foolish when the window was broken, but couldn't resist the impulse, and headed upstairs. She heard her son playing on the computer. She knocked on his door, and, when he called out, she sternly said, "Remember? Going to bed, waking up early, not gaming until midnight?"

He groaned. "Fine, I'm logging off."

She walked past his room and headed to hers. It was almost 10:00 p.m., and he should have been asleep already. But she had already too many things that she couldn't look after. On that note, she headed back to her mom's room, just to see her mom hadn't moved. She was sound asleep in bed, exactly as she'd seen her last, her pile of clothes on the floor. She picked them up, put them in the laundry hamper, and checked the toothbrush, but, of course, it was dry.

She also looked at the medications, wondering if she should wake up her mom to get them down, but, from the heavy snoring going on, she wasn't sure it was worth it. It was one more thing to talk to her doctor about because, if she couldn't get the medications down, that would be another argument for putting her in a home. Hating the decision-making that made her feel like a traitor to her own family, she slowly walked to her bedroom, where she completed her nightly ritual and then collapsed in bed.

Her last thought was about Harley and how little he'd changed. He looked so much the same, like when she'd last seen him, that it was almost a shock. He was a good man. She understood more about why he'd left, but, more than that, she understood just how young she'd been. Him too. And after eleven years raising a son on her own had shown her, it was the right thing for Harley to have done.

She needed to remember to tell him that, so that he could ease up on his own guilt too. He didn't have anything to feel guilty about. But she sure as hell did.

HARLEY HAD EXITED the truck and disappeared into the woods. After checking in with Badger, who had sent him a satellite image of the compound, Harley had done a Google search. Then he'd driven past the property. It was close to forty acres, with a series of buildings in the front, almost like offices, and various houses farther behind all that.

Now he parked a good mile from the compound. He left his truck and walked closer, as he studied the area. The moon was high; visibility was good. It was a perfect night to do a little bit of reconnaissance. As he approached, he saw a wired fence all around. He wasn't sure if it was electric or not. He opened his pocketknife, threw it gently, and immediately the fence zapped and sent off sparks. He sent Badger a text. **Electric fences.**

Of course, Badger responded. **They really don't want anybody in there.**

Just drugs?

I don't know about just drugs, he texted, **but obviously there's something, and they want to keep it secret.**

Got it. Just as he went to put away his phone, Badger sent back another quick message.

Take care, and don't get shot.

Harley thought about the forty acres, the location right up against the Canadian border, and how easy it would be to disappear into an area like this.

"That's the truth. Don't get shot."

He walked around the perimeter of the fenced area for the next hour, checking out what appeared to be a couple guys sitting at particular focal points, but no walking sentries, no dogs loose. If they depended mostly on the electric fence, they were foolish because there were all kinds of ways to get around and under it—not easily but definitely doable. Particularly since trees had grown up fast and had spanned over it.

A couple trees Harley could jump from and into the compound, but he had to have a way back out again, and that was a little bit more difficult. He also found a washout where a creek had gone through, and the bed itself at high water was probably fairly deep. Stealthily, he continued his walk all the way around. It was midnight by the time he finally made his way back around to his truck.

All he had learned was that nobody was on guard at any set points. He'd come across two people talking, with a couple dogs, who hadn't even heard his arrival. But they sat in a hunting blind, using it as a lookout, which was convenient for them, not so much for him. But he'd spotted them because of the noise they made. If they'd been quiet, Harley wouldn't have known about their presence, and they would have seen him first.

As it was, he marked it on his map and kept on going. Finally, by the time he was done, he sent a copy of the map and the blind to Badger, stating that he'd done a full circle around the inner fenced-in area but wasn't finding anything overtly suspicious here. He also asked if Badger had access to a drone. Harley would love to get some aerial images.

We can use the satellite and maybe get you something closer, Badger replied. **A drone they're likely to see.**

Maybe, Harley texted. **But, if it's small enough, they might miss it.**

Badger wrote, **We might consider getting one, but we can't make it too expensive. You're likely to have it destroyed in the process.**

Harley couldn't argue with that. **I'll see what's in town**, he texted. **I might have to order one in.**

That's possible too.

With that, they left the discussion until more research could be done. As he was about to get into his vehicle, he saw a very climbable tree off to the side. Not hesitating, he locked the truck back up, walked over to the tree, and climbed as high as he could. From here, he had a great vantage point, where he could look across the compound. The first of many buildings sat just in the front, lights all out, and looked unoccupied.

In the distance, he saw several houses. He wasn't sure if this property had once been multiple titles that had all been bought up, but usually you weren't allowed more than a certain number of houses on a property without classifying it as commercial. And this definitely wasn't zoned for commercial use.

On the other hand, if this drug operation had people here, whoever was running this place needed to have residences for everybody. People coming and going caused comment, and shopping locally in town would have brought more comments as well. Chances were, they had to get everything trucked in.

And that was something else Harley noted for himself. He had also seen a double gate and a sentry at the gate that he'd driven past on his way here. He hadn't seen anybody who appeared to notice him driving by, but he knew, if he came back a second time, that this black truck would get noticed. He made a note to change out his rental tomorrow. He took several photographs, which would allow him at least to keep track of where the lights were because he saw several lights in the darkness. And they were likely to be houses or some kind of work facility.

He wondered just how close he was to the Canadian border.

And that was another question that he sent to Badger. **How close to the Canadian side are we?** When there was no answer, Harley figured Badger had probably gone to sleep, which should have been a while ago. Kat was pregnant and probably struggling to get enough sleep as it was. When Harley finally crawled back down the tree, he was feeling remarkably decent about what he'd seen. Now what he hadn't found though was the dog.

On that note, he had a dog whistle with him that he'd picked up from a friend who had military connections, and he sent out a whistle, superhigh, that most people wouldn't note, but it should set the dog on edge. He didn't want to hurt him with the piercing sound, but, at the same time, he wanted the dog to be aware that he was out here and was coming for him. A bark came from the distance, which made him smile. He sent out a short burst on the whistle and then another short burst. At least then the dog would know when he got closer, if he used the same pattern.

On that note, he climbed back into his truck and drove past the property—without the truck's headlights on—and then turned the lights back on when he got into town and drove up to the pub. The pub itself was rocking and rolling pretty heavily, but Harley slipped past everybody and headed upstairs to his room. Only as he paused in the hallway did one of the staff call out, "There was a phone call for you earlier. Did you get it?"

"No. Do you know who it was?"

"She didn't leave a message," the woman said, "but I think it was Jasmine." She gave him a knowing grin. "And, of course, you know her pretty well, don't you?"

He didn't say anything, just thanked her politely and headed for his room. Did everybody treat her like that for the last eleven, twelve years? He wanted to punch somebody for it. Especially when nobody, it seemed, knew the truth or even cared enough to find out the truth.

Another woman stepped into view. "Harley?" She studied him, making sure.

Harley frowned, then grinned. "Diane?"

They both chuckled.

"You've changed," Diane noted. "Grew into a man while

in the navy."

Harley nodded, pointing at her pregnant belly. "And you grew into a wife and mother."

Diane's laughter lit up the hallway. "Best thing I've done, since marrying Daniel."

"You and he both look very happy."

"We *are* very happy. There's a difference."

Harley agreed. "That's the best kind of relationship. But … what are you doing up past midnight?"

"Walking." She grinned. "This one keeps me up all hours of the night. Daniel won't let me go driving around in the dark solo, so I move the baby around by walking. Seems to calm the baby, so I can sleep eventually."

Harley shook his head. "Pregnancy is a different world, right? Do you know the sex of the baby?"

Diane smiled broadly. "We do this time. The first two we wanted to be surprised. But, with the bedroom shortage at our home, and the differences in this pregnancy from my first two, I think we're having a girl. Our next doctor's visit will confirm it, one way or another."

"Congratulations."

"Oh, that's right. You haven't met our boys. We should invite you over before you leave, so you can see them firsthand." She waved him off, as she headed the other way. "And Jasmine is invited too."

"Diane," Harley called out, stopping her. "Do you think Daniel would mind if I helped myself to some raw hamburger meat?" At her curious stare, he added, "I'll pay you back, buy more meat to replace it, later tomorrow—which is today. I might need it."

Diane gave him a long look then disappeared into the back. Ten minutes later, the meat loaded into his truck,

Harley heading for a closer look at the property in question. He enjoyed the drive. Too bad it was used for a drug op. It could be so much more out here. With a shake of his head, he parked two miles away, farther than the scope of any known cameras set up at the compound.

Harley mentally reviewed his plan to access the compound. The easiest would be to jump into the compound, over the electric fence, via a couple tall trees that spanned over the fence itself. That would also likely give him the fastest exit if he were chased by dogs or gunmen. If he'd brought enough rope …

Granted, he wanted to avoid the dogs if at all possible but knew he probably couldn't, the meat would at least deter the dogs from attacking him.

With his night vision goggles, he would have preferred a partner in person, someone as his backup, but he didn't figure anyone other than Daniel in town would deign to pair up with Harley, as damaged as his reputation had become. And Harley refused to put Daniel in any danger with the upcoming birth of his third child.

He grabbed the rope, hooking it over one shoulder, with the bagged meat in a duffel bag thrown over his other shoulder. He hiked the two miles to his chosen position and scaled the best tree for the job. Tying his rope off on a limb strong enough to handle his weight, he dropped to the ground.

Without the rope, he had cut the weight of his baggage in half. He kept to the trees, nearing the office buildings. Thankfully no lights were on in any of these buildings—at least not that he saw from the front.

The biggest building had no windows. That was disappointing. Jogging to the other smaller nearby buildings,

Harley checked out the windows in each. Thankfully the moonlight and the dirt-free windows helped Harley make out what was inside. One building was totally storage, full of unmarked boxes. One building looked just like a lab. *Fitting for a drug op*, he thought. Another building housed four-wheeled vehicles, basically a garage. Yet another building served as a huge pantry, full of canned goods and bags of staples—flour, sugar, dried beans, rice, potatoes, onions, *dog food.*

At that finding, Harley heard the pitter-patter of a four-legged animal. *Damn.* He bolted to the far side heading back to his dangling rope.

Until he ran into a dog coming straight at him.

Accessing the ground meat, he dropped several chunks in the opposite direction of where he was going and backed up enough to turn and race toward his exit.

Then someone appeared. Thankfully he was alone. No dog with him. Harley stilled, counted off three minutes to make sure the guy was out of hearing before Harley climbed his tree. That done, he untied the rope, climbed down the tree, jogged again to his truck. Harley drove back to town, watching for any unwanted company behind him.

There was no sign of anyone. Harley let out a sigh of relief, unloaded his rental truck, and headed for his shower.

CHAPTER 5

JASMINE GOT UP the next morning at seven, as was her usual schedule, made coffee, and heard her son racing down the stairs. He raced into the kitchen, gave her a quick hug, bussed her on the cheek. "I have to run."

"And no breakfast again." Her tone was dry.

He grinned, grabbed a couple granola bars. "I'll eat these after basketball, but I have to go." And, just like that, he flew out of the house.

She shook her head. She didn't know when he had become such a busy person, but his life was filled with sports and friends. She could get behind that because he had good friends, but, at the same time, she also knew that friends could turn on him. She hadn't had a whole lot of friends because they couldn't come over and partake in any sports or games at her house. And everybody thought to have her foster brother around was also weird; yet more than that was nobody liked her parents either.

As she thought about it, she realized just how much control her parents had had over her life, and, by getting pregnant as early as she had, she'd fallen right into the same control pattern. She walked up and knocked on her mom's room, and, when there was no answer, she pushed it open to see her mom snoring gently. It was still early, so Jasmine went back downstairs and sat outside with her coffee. She needed to decide what she would do about her future. Get a job, retrain, something, because in less than seven years her son would be done with high school and then off to college.

What he would do, she didn't know, but he was talking about engineering. She also didn't know how student loans worked because his college fees were another thing beyond her ability to pay for on her own. And that just made her feel even worse as a parent. She knew that most parents couldn't pay for the astronomical education requirements, but, at the same time, she wanted to do something. She hadn't been good at anything but graphics. She had dallied around with things like that, wondering about going into something related, like creating digital book covers, promotions, banners, and things like that, but didn't know if there was any job market for it.

She had done a little bit before, but nothing that ever made her any money. And who could she even talk to about it? It was just one of those things that never seemed to get any easier to figure out. She was in a rut. A rut that had encompassed staying at home way longer than she should have. But what were her choices? First, it had been her pregnancy, then her father's death, and, well, taking care of her baby and now her mother. But she had her whole life ahead of her, and she didn't want that to be defined by her world now. Other things were out there for her. She just had to figure it out. She wasn't sure how to do that.

As she sat here pondering, she got a text message from Harley.

Can you all go out for breakfast?

She smiled, wishing she could. And then texted back

Mom's still asleep. Jimmy's at tryouts at school already. Breakfast at your place?

She laughed out loud. **Most people wait until they're invited.**

You probably won't invite me, he wrote back.

She frowned at that because, of course, she would invite him. If anything, he was a link to her happier time in life. And yet why was that? Except that, as she realized he'd stayed because of her, she had also had an easier time because of him. They had both spent as much time as they could together, and, as a parent, she realized how much that must have infuriated her father. She shook her head because parenting her son gave her quite a different view on her own parents.

And maybe they'd had a right to be so worried; she didn't know, but her father had been obviously just as equally guilty for the strained relationship that they'd all had. She couldn't blame him for everything though. Her mom had played a role in that too.

Jasmine shook her head. "No point getting upset about any of it now," she muttered to herself. "It's been over for a long time." She sent back a message. **Yes, come for breakfast.** And then smiled when she got a happy face in response. There was just something so full of life about having Harley back in her world. It was dangerous, more than dangerous given the circumstances, but she wasn't a sixteen-year-old to get pregnant.

On the other hand, neither was she on birth control, and that was something that made her stop and think. She never really thought about it before because she hadn't had a full-time boyfriend. And getting pregnant the way she had then had completely stopped her from dating in all the years since. Sex was also a mystery. She'd conceived a child but had no memory of her one and only sexual encounter. She'd shut down after that party, and the consequences of life had taken over.

Besides, nobody wanted to be around her and her parents, and nobody wanted to be around her raising a child. She had essentially isolated herself by circumstances. Maybe if she hadn't been quite so choosy, she would have been more open to dating opportunities, but she *was* choosy and didn't think that she had to stop being choosy in order not to be alone. And besides, she wasn't alone. She had her son, and that made up for so much in her world.

She was still sitting here and pondering life's mysteries, when a knock came on the door. She hopped to her feet and walked there, checking through the living room window first. Seeing Harley, she opened up the door and stepped aside. "You didn't waste any time," she murmured, glancing at the white truck he drove now. She frowned, pointed.

"Had to change it out," he stated, without further explanation. "There's nothing colder than a pub in the morning. Plus, I didn't want to be there for breakfast either. I think Daniel and his family have most of their breakfasts there, with Daniel cooking, from what I understand. So I thought I could go down to the big Pancake House that's around the corner, and that's when I invited you all."

"But I can't leave Mom, and she's still asleep."

"Right. I forgot how much she has changed." He gave a good natured shrug, as if to say, *Whatever.*

She nodded. "And I understand if you don't want to be here."

"I didn't say that. You invited me for breakfast. I'm here."

She snorted. "Well, you invited yourself for breakfast."

"And hopefully I'm welcome." He quietly studied her.

"Of course you are," she replied immediately, feeling terrible. "I figured that you would be out looking for the dog."

"I was. I was out at midnight last night, then again this morning," he told her. "After I eat, I'll go back again."

"But what can you do?" she asked.

"Breach their electric fence," he admitted, "to find that War Dog."

She stared at him in shock. "They have an electric fence?"

"Yes, and that's very suspicious."

"Well, if it's drugs they're running, maybe not."

"The other thing is, it seems their forty-acre property butts up against the border."

"Well, we are just like nine miles away. So you think that maybe they're crossing the US-Canadian border to buy or sell drugs?"

"A small town is on the other side. So that's possible."

"So maybe you need to contact the Canadians."

"My boss is doing that, but meanwhile I was thinking about food, and that's when I started on this pathway."

"Right." She smirked. "Come on in. I could use a good meal."

"And what do you normally have for breakfast? What does *a good meal* mean to you?"

"I have sausage and eggs," she replied, "and some hash brown patties, if you're really hungry."

"Yes, to all three, please." He rubbed his tummy. "Any chance of toast too?"

She laughed. "I have a French bread here that we can slice up." They quickly cut through the living room into the kitchen, where she started prepping breakfast.

"Did you wake up your mom?"

"Not yet, but I need to. However, she hasn't been sleeping all that well lately, so now that she's had a good night, I don't want to disturb her too much."

"So maybe let's have breakfast and then see?"

"Maybe. I don't know. It's frustrating. I never quite know what to do. If I wake her, then I feel like I've disturbed her rest, especially if she gets cranky. If I don't wake her, and she wakes up cranky, I feel like I should have woken her up earlier." She laughed. "I'm always second-guessing myself."

"You've done a good job, you know?" he said quietly.

She jerked her head toward him and frowned. "I'm surprised you say that. You haven't been around here to see if I have or not."

"No, but you've held it together, and that's more than a lot of people can say. You've stuck by the job for over a decade, and that's also more than a lot of people have done." He added, "You've raised your son and done a hell of a nice job. He's a good-looking young man. He's polite. He cleans up after himself, and he gets to eat well because you have plenty of food for him. He just seems to be a together kid."

"He reminds me of you in a lot of ways. And yet I don't know why because he's not your son and because you were a very angry teen for a lot of those years."

"I was angry because of the restrictions and the power your father had over me. It's one of the reasons why, in the navy, I dove into self … into weapons and self-defense. Once you lose power or you never had a chance to gain power and then you do get it, it's important that you control it with a clear head."

"Yes," she admitted. "I imagine it's something that's really hard to let go of."

"Did you have any control when your son was born?"

"It's one of the things that I fought long and hard for. I didn't tell my parents, until after it was past the abortion period, because they would have insisted on that. Then they tried to insist that I adopt out the child, and I refused." She shook her head. "It was my son. I didn't know if I would have any other children in this lifetime, and, since my parents only had me, they finally broke down and accepted my decision—only because I was having a boy. Of course a male was so much more important than … than their daughter. If nothing else, I had at least produced a grandson for them." She snorted. "Dad was confused and mixed up about it all. But I think he did love Jimmy."

"Well, that would have been a redeeming factor for him." Harley tried to hold back his sarcasm.

"Right? When I look back at the childhood we both had, you were the foster child, and I was the biological child, but I'm not sure either of us were well treated."

"Neither of us were, then taking half my wages too."

"I was talking to my son about that last night. I took on a lot of babysitting and daycare when he was little. And my mother insisted on getting half of that money too."

He stared at her. "Even though you needed it for your own son?"

"Well, back when they were both alive, my parents considered that, because my son would be living here at their home, that I should be paying room and board. And the trouble is, they were also right," she murmured. "I wasn't paying my way, so …"

He shook his head. "I mean, I guess, in one sense, helping out with room and board is to be expected, and a lot of parents would consider something like that if their adult child comes home with another child. In this situation, you were too young to have all that responsibility foisted on you. They should have helped you, not the other way around."

"Well, I would have appreciated that mind-set from any adult. However, I went from feeling like a victim and feeling guilty to *being* a victim and *being* guilty."

Very quickly they had a hot breakfast and toast. She sat down. "Now let's hope I get to eat this before Mom wakes up."

He winced at that. "And, of course, she has to be looked after immediately, doesn't she?"

"Well, it depends. Sometimes she wakes up, dresses, and comes downstairs, all completely normal. Although she often doesn't know whose kitchen it is or who I am, she's capable of at least getting that far. And sometimes she just stays in bed and cries for help."

"WOW. I DON'T think I would have the patience." Harley glanced at the staircase.

"Maybe not. … There are times when I'm not sure I do either, but I have to consider what the other alternative is."

"You already know what it is."

Jasmine nodded. "I'm just not sure that I'm capable of doing that."

"You'll work it out," he stated comfortably.

She smiled. "What's your plan of action now with the dog?"

He pulled out a whistle. "This is a dog whistle that's used in the military. I was using it last night and first thing this morning, trying to alert the dog that I'm around. Of course the other dogs at the compound will hear the dog whistle, but only the War Dog will understand the various kinds of whistles. So he'll be a little more aware when I come up to him."

"Interesting. Will he trust that loyalty more than what he's currently been exposed to?"

"Maybe. I've also got to visit with the guy who sold him."

"Oh, that should be fun. Because, if he sold the dog voluntarily, then surely that's not something he wants to disclose."

"Won't get a choice either way. These War Dogs? … There's a government contract they sign, promising to keep them in good shape and to look after them, and, if you have a problem and can't look after them, then you're supposed to contact the War Department."

"Well, I'm glad to hear that, but you just have to make sure you look after you too, especially if you keep going back to that compound," she murmured.

He finished off his breakfast, snatched the last piece of toast, and looked at her, one eyebrow raised. She shook her head. "Go. Eat up," she replied. "I imagine, when you left here, all you did was eat."

"I did, but I also was into heavy physical workouts, and I put on a ton of muscle."

"You're way bigger than I remember." She studied his shoulders.

"And I've lost a lot since the injury."

"You haven't explained what happened."

"Not a whole lot to tell. We were involved in official war games, as part of our training, when I was injured. A piece of essential equipment failed." He shrugged. "I lost my arm."

He held up the glove on his left hand, and her eyes opened wide, and she gasped. "Oh, I didn't even notice."

He smiled, pulled the glove off his fingers, and showed her his prosthetic lower arm and fingers that moved quite smoothly.

She shook her head. "Oh, my God. You were really badly hurt."

"Well, I lost most of the arm and a whole lot of muscle and got a titanium knee and hip," he noted, with a smile. "But, all in all, I'm still me."

"Hell no, you're not the same in any way. You're a hell of a lot better than you ever were. And that's something you need to remember."

He looked at her, beaming. "Thank you. I'll take that as a compliment."

"And that's because it was. You're definitely improved over the angry, sad, hungry young man you were."

"Is that good or bad?"

She gave him a cheeky smile. "Oh, I loved that one, so I certainly don't have any problem with this version."

CHAPTER 6

JASMINE WAS SHOCKED when she realized the extent of Harley's injuries. And knowing that he was injured and heading off to deal with this dog and whatever else might be at the compound just made her even more worried. She asked him, "Do you have a plan?"

"Yep, we'll see if I can take the place of a delivery driver today and get onto the compound."

"And then what?"

He gave her a mysterious smile. "Then we'll see." She protested, but he'd gently stroked her cheek in a move that made her stop instantly and stare up at him. "I'll be fine."

She shook her head. "You've been in scenarios where you weren't fine." She pointed at his left arm. "Otherwise you wouldn't have gotten so badly injured. How can you tell me that you'll be fine in that tone of voice and then just walk away?"

"The dog needs to be looked after."

She shrugged. "I get that. I really do, but it's also important that you look after you."

He burst out laughing. "For the last couple years all I've done is look after me. From surgery to rehab and recovery, it's been only about me. Now it's time to turn around and to give back, so it's about others too."

She watched him walk out the door, her arms crossed

over her chest, struggling to deal with the fact that he was in her life again and a powerful force at that. It had always been like that for the two of them. It's like he came into this world, and there was no room for anything else.

She'd loved it because he'd filled every corner of her emptiness back then. And now? Here he was doing it all over again. As she stood here, watching the street long after he drove away, she heard her mother calling. She bowed her head for a long moment and then closed the front door and walked up the stairs. She walked inside her mother's bedroom, and her mom was lying in bed, smiling up at her. "Good morning, Mom."

"Good morning, Jasmine. How was your night?"

At that, Jasmine's heart lightened. Her mom had had a good night and was having a good morning because she remembered her daughter's name. Jasmine gave her a gentle kiss. "I'm fine. You ready to get up?"

"Yes, I am, and I'm really hungry." She threw back the bedcovers, stood, and made her way shakily to the bathroom while Jasmine watched.

On her good days, she got quite irritated if Jasmine treated her as an invalid, and offering help was one of those no-no things. When her mother came back out again, she headed straight for the wardrobe. "I feel like wearing something bright and sunny today."

"Do you want any help?" And then Jasmine immediately winced.

Her mother turned to her and frowned. "Why would I need any help getting dressed?" She shook her head. "Go put on the coffee," she ordered. "I'm really hungry."

"There might still be some sausages and eggs."

"Oh, I don't want leftover eggs," she replied, a moue

puckering her face. "But sausages would be good."

"I can fry a couple fresh eggs for you," she offered.

Her mother immediately nodded. "That sounds perfect, plus a piece of toast."

Jasmine dashed down the stairs, a big smile on her face because, if there was one thing to make her heart feel good, it was to have a conversation with her mother and to know that her mother was actually in there. The rest of the time, it was just deadly to face the Alzheimer's again and again. Jasmine worked away at cooking fresh eggs for her mom. When she turned to reach for a plate, she caught sight of somebody staring over the fence at her.

She stared in shock and then immediately stepped out of view. She didn't know who it was, and she didn't want to. Except … that's where Harley had determined the shooter was. Like a mama bear, Jasmine's protective streak emerged. She quickly put the eggs onto a plate. And, staying out of sight, put the pan back down, shut off the burner, and stepped outside through the glass sliding doors, where she was still out of sight but could see him.

She pulled up her phone and took a photo of him. And then she heard barking. She headed inside again to the spare room and looked out the window. And this same guy was walking outside their wooden fence but a little farther along the road, now reaching a chain-link fence, so she saw a great big shepherd at his side on a big chain leash with a great big choker around its neck.

She frowned at that and took another photo and pondered if she should show them to Harley or the deputy. For that matter. She didn't know whether her friend Chester might be interested in it, and, on the other hand, he might say it has nothing to do with them. When the guy came around the front of her house and stepped up her porch steps, she boldly faced him and asked him if there was something he needed.

"Yes," he nodded. But then he wouldn't tell her what it was.

She looked down at the dog, who looked up at her. "Is that a War Dog?'

Immediately the guy stiffened and jerked on the chain. The dog gave a small yelp, and she winced. "You don't have to be mean."

"I'm not being mean"—he glared at her—"but he needs to learn to obey."

"You won't get anywhere with force and fear," she snapped. "If you can't keep the dog in good condition and good health, then give him to somebody else."

"I paid damn good money for this animal," he sneered. "No way in hell I'm letting anybody else have him."

"So that is the War Dog that's gone missing, huh?" she sneered right back. "And the Defense Department's looking for him."

He immediately stared at her in shock. "What the hell do you even know about this?"

"More than you do obviously," she replied. "You should just put him in the fence right here in my backyard and leave the dog, before the government comes down on your case."

"The dog's going nowhere," he stated in a defiant mood.

"I've already got pictures of you and him. And sent them on to the Defense Department," she snapped. He glared at her and instantly a handgun appeared in his fist. She noted it, surprised as her rage snapped to the forefront. "Yeah. What's your world all about?" she asked. "Keeping scary dogs at your side and a handgun? And what am I? Just a defenseless woman, and you're scared of me."

"I'm not fucking scared of you," he snapped. "What's to be scared of?"

"You're the one standing here with a dog that you can't control and a gun pointed in my direction," she answered. "Wait until the Defense Department finds out about that."

"You want to die?"

"Not really." She stiffened her back and glared at him. "But what I won't do is let you turn that dog into a mean, nasty, vicious animal because you keep abusing it."

His fist yanked on the tether to the dog, and the dog yelped again.

"See? You're such a shitty owner that you can't even control the dog without hurting him."

"This dog is mine, and you don't get a right to tell me how to look after it."

"No, but the Defense Department does," she stated smoothly, "and you have no business even having that animal."

"I paid damn good money for him. Nobody'll take him away from me."

"We'll see about that … because whoever it was who sold him to you had no right to sell him, and that was something that the US government is already aware of, so they're coming after you." She studied him. "As I said, you should just put the dog somewhere safe, so they don't come back and check out the rest of your little operation."

At that, his gaze turned hard, and he glared at her. He pointed the gun at her face. "You better watch your mouth," he growled, "before those around you don't get to wake up one morning."

"And now we have death threats. Thank you. More

ammunition to get your ass hauled off the street and tossed into jail."

He shook his head. "I don't understand what the hell is wrong with you."

"I don't know where it's coming from either today, but I'm damn tired of being a victim."

He sneered. "I know something about you that you don't know. So I suggest that, before you get too mouthy and think that you're too high on the hog for the rest of us, I know exactly where your son came from."

And, with that, he gave a bark of laughter and disappeared around the corner.

HARLEY SPOKE TO the delivery driver outside the grocery store. He looked at him, smiled. "I understand you're heading up to the Consalus place."

The guy immediately froze. "Yeah, we do deliveries there twice a week." He looked over at him, stared him up and down. "Why?"

"Do you always go alone?"

He nodded. "That's the only way they let me on the place."

"So, if I wanted to get onto the place, how would I do it?"

"I wouldn't do it at all, if I were you. Pretty sure they shot the last trespasser."

"Not surprised, but a dog is there that they don't have the rights to."

He studied him. "Man, you don't want to get yourself shot over a dog."

"Nope, I sure don't, but neither do they get to keep the dog. It's a US War Dog, who gave years of his life to serve for the military and was not supposed to end up in the hands of thugs, like these guys."

"I remember that dog. He's a big one. Scary. The guy walks him around town all the time."

"Interesting. I'd like to see him and the dog."

"He's in town right now. I think I saw him downtown when I came through. Don't ask me to take you inside the compound again, please. I've got enough troubles. They already make my life hell, and I have this big long set of security questions I have to answer. If they find out I'm lying, it's bad news."

Immediately Harley nodded. "Wouldn't want to do that to you. I'd like to see that downtown area they walk, but I'd sure like to get onto the compound too."

"At least twenty guys are out there, and they're all armed. You might get in through the gate one day, but, even if you got into the compound, it won't do you any good. Far better you show up with the sheriff or the military and take the dog that way. Especially if it's a War Dog, you should have military backing behind you."

"It'll take something like that to get him out?"

"Absolutely it will."

Harley watched, stepping back, until the delivery guy was loaded up, and he let him go ahead, Harley following him. Harley didn't want to get him into any trouble, but the delivery guy was right. There had to be a way to get onto the property or to just to see the dog and to separate the dog while this guy was out and about in downtown. As the delivery guy drove through the downtown area, he honked at Harley and pointed out his open window, down a street.

Harley immediately turned down that street and came upon a series of warehouses. Outside one were a couple dogs, their owners talking. Then he realized that they weren't owners as much as handlers. He pulled off to the side and pretended to be looking at his GPS, as if lost. They didn't even seem to notice him. He pulled the whistle from his pocket and used it. Both dogs lifted their ears and turned and looked in his direction. The second dog stepped to the side, a great big choke collar around its neck. That dog looked to be the perfect image of the War Dog he was looking for. He smiled. "It's okay, boy. We're coming to get you."

This one, Bowser, looked like he was in decent health. But, even as the dog turned to look at him, his handler jerked hard on the dog's leash, his neck pulled, while a shock also went through his system. The dog yelped, and Harley saw the tremors going up and down his legs. Harley's anger grew at that. Shock collars were meant to be training tools and rarely used in the military.

For the dog, it would have been a hell of a problem. But the handler had the controller in his other hand and appeared to be buzzing it just because he felt like it.

As soon as he finished his conversation with the other guy, the two parted and kept walking. Then Harley realized that they weren't even talking so much as it was a sentry break. And they kept walking around the property of that one warehouse. He sat here and waited until they made it back around again. Fourteen minutes for one pass.

He studied the building and then quickly sent info on it and a picture of it to Badger, asking if he knew anything about the building. It had two sentries keeping watch, plus Bowser and the second dog.

Badger texted back that he would find out and would contact the local sheriff's department.

Harley looked at that last text and thought about the local authorities in this rural area and realized not much would be here. A sheriff and maybe a deputy or two, but that was about it. Still, they might have something on record for problems at this address. He got out of his newest rental and walked down the block on his own, studying the buildings on the opposite side. One of the sentries didn't like him even that close, and he yelled at him. Harley turned.

The guy snapped, "What are you doing here?"

He took in his features, cataloguing the man. "Just looking at these properties."

"We don't like people hanging around. Get in your vehicle and get lost."

He stopped, stared. "Why? What are you protecting?"

At that, the guy shut up and glared at him, but he nudged the dog forward. The dog looked at Harley and growled. But Harley checked the dog, not the one he was interested in. "It's okay, boy. I'm not doing anything at all."

"He doesn't fucking care if you do or not. He follows my orders, not yours," the sentry snapped.

"Sounds like you don't deserve to have a dog at all. You don't raise them with fear."

"We raise them whatever way we want to raise them, and you can't do anything about it."

"Maybe, maybe not, but one has to give it some good consideration."

"That's BS."

"Besides, if you guys weren't so damn scared of somebody getting into whatever you're protecting over there, it wouldn't be a big deal."

"We didn't say we're protecting anything."

"Oh, come on. Gimme a break. Two of you walking around one building? If you were looking after the entire area, the whole block, it'd be a different story because your security route would be different. But, no, you're right there at this corner."

The guy looked at him. "You don't know nothing about this building. If you're smart, you'll forget about it."

And, for all this confrontation with this guy, this wasn't the man with the right dog. "Where's your buddy?" Harley asked him.

"Watching you," he sneered. "Do you really think we aren't keeping an eye on everybody here?"

"Makes me wonder why." He studied the building. "Warehouse for drugs, perhaps?"

The smile fell off the guy's face. "You don't know anything."

"Nope, obviously not. Interesting what's going on here though."

"Well, you should stop being interested in anything here," said a stranger beside Harley.

Harley turned to see the dog that he was interested in and a handler who was already angry at seeing Harley. "And there's the War Dog." Harley nodded to the shepherd right in front of him. "Nice job on taking him off the other guy's hands."

"I don't know anything about a War Dog," he replied nervously. "I bought and paid for this dog in good faith."

"Doesn't matter if you did or not." He wondered though at the man's wariness. "Not only are you abusing him, particularly with that series of studded collars—in reverse, of all things—but, if you can't control a well-trained dog, which this one is, without abusing him, what the hell are you doing with any animal?"

"He's my dog. You're not touching him." His fist tightened on the dog's chain leash.

"I'll take him if I want to," Harley stated, with a hard tone. "Fact of the matter is, he's not yours to manhandle like that." He took a step forward.

Immediately the guy stepped back with the dog. "I'll turn him loose on you."

"Feel free. Depends on how long you've had him whether you've trained him to be ugly enough or not."

"He'll rip you to pieces," the other guy shouted at him.

Harley looked over at the other sentry. That dog growled. Harley turned toward Bowser and used a hand signal. The dog cocked his head at him in confusion.

"What did you do?" the punk asked.

"Nothing."

Harley looked at the War Dog. "Hey, Bowser."

Bowser's ears immediately pulled together, and he whined. Harley gave him a *halt and stand* order. Immediately the dog's butt hit the deck, and he looked up at him, waiting for the next order. Harley nodded. "I'll be taking that dog off of you right now."

"You and whose army?" he sneered, pulling back hard on the dog's neck. The dog growled, which turned quickly to a howl of pain.

Harley didn't wait. He jumped forward and, with his right fist, clocked the handler in the jaw. He went down without a sound. Harley immediately bent down, even though the other man was shouting and screaming at him and holding a gun, pointed at him. Harley looked over at him and immediately released all the collars off Bowser, then told him immediately to heel. Bowser immediately raced into the heel position. He was confused but not unhappy about the turn of events.

Harley stood and looked at the other guy. "Hand over your dog."

"Like fuck I will," he snapped. "I don't know what the hell you just did, but you're not taking my dog."

"Obviously you don't know how to work your dog, and I don't know where he came from, but, if you keep abusing him, I'll make sure you lose him anyway."

"I didn't abuse him. I'm not abusing him. I don't use the collars, like he does."

"That's a damn good thing, but, if I ever see you hurting that dog, you'll lose him. Permanently."

"You can't fucking tell me what to do," he sneered. "And this isn't my dog. My boss will have your head."

"It's not his dog either. If he wants him, he can come and get them." Harley straightened, widening his stance. "This dog belongs to the US Defense Department. He spent his life saving soldiers at war. The last thing he needed was to get in the hands of a psychopath, like your buddy here."

"He did have some issues handling him. He was using it more as a status symbol, trying to curry favor with the boss."

"Well, it backfired. He got attention all right, but not the kind that'll do him any good."

The nervous guy with the gun looked down at his buddy. "Did you kill him?"

"Nope, I didn't."

"You'll have to because he'll come after you now."

"Let him." Harley turned to stare at him. "Make sure you tell your boss too."

He looked at him, his gaze wide. "You got a death

wish?"

"Maybe. Any asshole who abuses a War Dog like this, he'll have me on his case. So go ahead and tell your boss because I presume he's the one who okayed the abuse in the first place."

"Not really. Boss is a little bit better with animals, but he expects well-trained people."

"Not my problem. Sounds like you guys don't have the training to look after these animals in the first place."

"That's not quite true, but this is way bigger than you."

"Of course it is," Harley snapped. "You're running drugs to Canada. I don't want any part of what you've got going on. But, if I ever see you hurt that dog, I don't care in what manner," he repeated, "you'll lose it."

The guy stepped back. "The dog isn't mine, and you'll take on more than you can chew if you try to take him right now."

Harley looked at the dog and gave a high-pitched whistle. The dog immediately stared up at him, his head cocked to the side. Harley gave him several hand signals, and the dog immediately followed orders. "So he was originally well trained, but you don't have the training to run them, do you?"

The guy looked uneasy. "Well, I've never had any experience with that."

"Yet the dog knows what the hell you're supposed to be doing, even if you don't," He gave the dog an order to come and to heel on the other side of Harley. Immediately the dog jumped forward, pulling free of the man's grasp, and coming around to sit down beside Harley. He stared at the handler. "As I told you, you don't have a clue."

"How did you do that?" He dropped his gun hand, staring at the dog and then back at Harley. "You don't understand. This is death for both of us."

"Or you could take a bus south and find another line of work."

"He'll find me." The nervous gunman was desperate. "You don't know what he's like."

"You're only brave," he snapped, "when you've got a gun or a dog like this beside you, but you can't even control it. You didn't even know what to do with him." In exasperation Harley studied the man, the boy, realizing his fear was real.

"You don't get it. Our boss won't handle this well. As in not very well at all. His temper is legendary."

"Depends whether his business is legit or not, but he really shouldn't be running dogs that none of you guys can handle."

"We handle them."

"No, you manhandle them," he clarified. "Don't ever think that what you were doing was handling them. As you can see, these dogs are trained and know exactly what you're supposed to be doing and can't figure out why the hell you're hurting them."

He stared down at the dog in shock. "We didn't mean to."

"I'm not so sure about that." Harley motioned at the man lying unconscious at his side. "Did you ever think that about him?"

"Some guys just like to hurt others. I like dogs. I don't use any of those spiked collars."

"No, but you were still pulling back on this one."

He flushed. "Yeah, because I didn't know how to make him do anything else."

"Well, maybe it's time for you to go into an industry where you know what you're doing."

The stranger shook his head. "This is what I'm in. You don't get out."

"If you move a long way away, you can."

"That's not so easy."

"I suppose he's got spies everywhere."

"No, not really. He's got an awful lot of enemies, but he's local and now trying to go big."

"Now that will just get him killed off too. The big guys are beyond big," Harley explained. "He doesn't know what he's trying to take on."

"No, maybe not, but he thinks he can do it, so ..." And he just shut up at that point.

"And you're okay getting killed in the line of your job?"

The guy shook his head slowly. "It shouldn't happen. Boss knows what he's talking about. He's smart and ambitious. He's got plans and can pull them off."

"Maybe. Maybe not."

He frowned, looked around. "I don't even know what I'm supposed to do right now. If I don't have the dog to go home with, it'll be bad news."

"Again, maybe it's time for you to crash your vehicle somewhere off a cliff and move south."

He looked at him in surprise. "You mean, like, fake my death and go?"

"Do you see any life for you right now?"

The guy slowly shook his head. "No, I don't, but that's your fault. You didn't have to do this. If you give me the dog, I'm safe."

Harley frowned. This scared kid was holding a gun, yet not thinking of it, much less using it. "Is your gun even loaded?"

The kid jerked, remembered the gun in his hand, but stayed mute.

"Why the hell do you carry one if you don't use it?" Harley shook his head. "Just like the dog, you shouldn't have a weapon. You pull that crap on another drug-runner, and you'll be shot dead. You hear me?"

The kid barely moved, but he seemed to be nodding.

"And what about this guy?"

He winced. "I don't know. This … That was his own personal dog. He might be okay."

"But he brought the dog into the fold as a favor, so how is it his dog?"

"I don't know. It's possible he can tell the boss that he stole it, and then the owner came and got the dog back again."

"And that'll just make him look weak."

"I know. I know, but that's not my fault. It's not my deal."

"I can't give you this dog back because you don't know how to run this animal."

The guy looked at him. "You could … You could show me."

At that, Harley stopped and stared. "You know what? If you were in any other industry but running drugs where this dog may turn against people, I might consider training you to properly handle *her*. But seeing as how all you want to do is run drugs and swing around guns and hurt others …"

"We've never had to hurt anybody," he replied desperately. "You don't understand. It's all for show."

"It's all for show until it's not," Harley declared. "The minute you have a weapon like that unloaded gun or these animals, they're only for show, until you run into trouble. And now that you've run into trouble, it's not that easy to get out of it. The minute somebody dies involving these dogs, not only is the dog getting shot and put down, but you'll be held for murder."

He looked up at him. "Then we're already too damn late."

"Have these dogs killed anyone?"

"The dogs, no." He then shut up and backed away. "Look. I don't know what I'll do, if you won't give me the dog. I don't have any choice but to tell him what you did."

"Go for it. Make sure you tell him that these dogs belong to the US Defense Department, and, if they want to bring on a war with the US military, they can fly at it," he noted smoothly.

The guy's eyes widened at that. He nodded, and he turned, and he bolted out of there. At that, Harley watched him disappear. He had both dogs and didn't have a clue who the second one was, but it had responded very well to its training. Now he had two dogs. He'd have to get them vet-checked, confirm the presence of microchips, and figure out where the second dog had come from. He already knew about Bowser's background.

But the other one? That was a surprise. Still, it was not some dog that he would leave for these assholes to ruin. He turned and looked down at the guy on the ground. "And what the hell's with you?" he muttered. But again he was out cold and wasn't up to giving any answers. Harley heard the sound of a siren, which a cruiser then came around the corner and stopped beside him. He turned to look at the sheriff's deputy but didn't recognize him and waited.

The guy came out, took one look. "What the hell's going

on here?"

"This guy picked a fight with his dog."

The officer looked at Harley. "What the hell?"

"Hey, I wouldn't just let him take me down, so I knocked him out."

The deputy looked at the dogs. "I know these dogs."

"Good. Then you also know that this one's a War Dog and belongs to the US Defense Department."

At that, the guy's eyebrows shot up. "Seriously?"

"Yes. This one's had similar training. I'll take it to the vet and get the microchip checked to see where and what's going on."

The deputy frowned, then dropped to the unconscious guy and got a good look at his face. "This guy's also got a record." He checked the guy's wallet and nodded. "Did he attack you?"

"He wouldn't listen, that's for sure, and he tried to sic the dog on me, so I plowed him one in the face."

He shook his head. "Where'd you learn to fight like that?"

"The navy." His voice was hard.

At that, the guy turned to face him. "Are you Harley?"

"I am, indeed." He studied the officer. "Who are you?"

"Chester. I was at Jasmine's place, last night over the shooting."

"Good. I wouldn't be at all surprised if this wasn't our shooter. And he has a handgun on him too."

At that, the deputy quickly searched the downed man and pulled out one weapon, plus an ankle piece. He shook his head. "Wow. He won't have licenses for these." Chester straightened. "I understand you have the bullet from Jasmine's wall."

Harley tilted his head. "I might."

"Hand it over. I'll need it to match to this weapon."

"Or we can turn over both to the nearest military facility."

"Hey, our ballistics are sent off to Bozeman. Hand over the bullet."

Harley shook his head. "Gotta clear it with Commander Glen Cross of the US Defense Department first."

"I'll be sending the gun to Bozeman. You want to gum up the works by holding back the bullet, you'll be hearing from us."

Harley was unmoved. He pointed at the prone guy on the sidewalk. "I think he works for your lovely little drug mess at the border there."

"That's where I saw him," Chester agreed quietly.

"You go over there much?" Harley's tone was soft, with an edge to it, as he studied the deputy.

Chester looked up at him. "Every once in a while we get some complaints. We try to keep an eye on it, but, so far, we haven't caught them with anything illegal."

"They had two guards doing rounds on this warehouse property behind me. You may want to check it out."

"Depending on what this altercation was all about, I might have grounds for that."

"I would highly suggest you do it regardless because I'm pretty sure a big stash is about to get moved from here."

He looked at him in surprise. "Why would you say that?"

"Because, for one, they had two guards walking the building, and, for two, the way the pair of men were acting was suspicious as hell, trying to run me away for standing here, looking across the street. But whatever you are going to do, you better do it fast because the handler of this second dog has taken off. I don't know if he'll survive or show up somewhere in a ditch. I told him that he should leave town, but these guys don't seem to get any smarter at this game."

"I don't suppose it was a young man, Mexican-looking, about twenty-five, twenty-six, with a big scar on his wrist?"

"Scar on the back of his hand and up to his arm, yes."

"Yeah, he's been in trouble a lot but nothing too serious."

"Until he got in touch with this group."

"Good point. I know his family."

"Well, if you know his family, you might want to tell them, or at least help them to get him out of town because, … once I took the dog away from him, he's running scared. He knows he'll be in trouble with his boss."

"*Trouble with the boss* is bad news for everybody. If he stays out of trouble, we leave him alone."

"So you know that there's drug-running going on at the Canadian border, and you're not doing anything?"

He glared at him. "Of course we're doing something. We're building a case against him."

"And I wonder about that too. Or is it just that he pours enough money into town that you don't rock the boat if there's no need?"

The deputy glared at him.

Harley held out his hands. "Hey, I'm just here on behalf of the War Dogs. If this is how you guys operate … and if I happen to pass along information regarding the drug-running to both US and Canadian authorities …"

"You're hardly one to talk. You're the one who left one of our poor local girls pregnant when you took off."

"You should have another talk with Jasmine about that

because, as much as I would be honored to have Jimmy as my son, he isn't."

At that, the deputy stepped back and looked at him in shock. "What?"

"And if anybody had listened to her back then, you would all know that she was date-raped at a local party."

Chester's face paled. "Jesus Christ, are you serious?"

"Very. But nobody, including her parents, would let her say anything, and those she did try to tell didn't believe her. So I'm pissed. And I'm here. And, if I can solve that one too, while I'm here, believe me. I will."

"Oh no, you don't," he said immediately. "None of this vigilante bullshit."

"Not bullshit. You guys didn't take care of your own. I had to leave because of her father. Always intended to come back, until I realized how many years had gone by," he admitted. "That's on me, but you guys didn't look after her either."

"None of us knew," he snapped.

"Somebody knew. I think a hell of a lot of people knew, but it was just easier to blame me. Well, I'm not a kid anymore, and nobody gets to blame me for something I didn't do."

The deputy stood back, rubbed his face. "What the hell? She didn't even report it."

"Are you sure about that? … She sure believes she did. She was only sixteen at the time. I think she also lives in fear that, whoever raped her, that asshole is still around."

"Why would you say that?"

"Because of the look on her face when she realized that there was a bullet through her kitchen window," he stated forcibly.

"Yeah, but that's because you're in town. You were always trouble."

"Yeah, maybe so. Because whoever did date-rape her and whoever did leave her pregnant and with a mess afterward to handle on her own, now knows that I'm home and can verify that it wasn't my child, which means it's somebody else's."

"Every girl's allowed to make a mistake."

"Her? *She* made a mistake?"

Chester stopped, frowned. "You're getting me confused. Don't mess … Don't twist my meaning."

Harley stalked over to Chester, nose to nose. Chester took another step back. Harley leaned in. "You're supposed to be her friend as well as a deputy. I won't tell her what just spewed out of your mouth, but you can damn well bet that I won't forget it. So let me set you straight. And if you listen well enough, I won't have to report you to the sheriff or to the county DA or to the state AG or to the fucking DOJ. So listen up, *Chester*. If she went to a party and was given a date-rape drug or was knocked out and raped because of it, that's not on her. That's on the asshole who did this. I'm back. I know for a fact that it's not my child. And you can damn well believe that whoever raped her back then, if he's still around, will know there will be shit hitting the fan right now."

Chester swallowed hard, then finally finding his voice, said, "He might think that it was yours anyway."

"He might, but you can bet I'd be taking a DNA test right now and proving that it wasn't."

With a wary eye on Harley, Chester seemed to put the two together. "You're thinking that's what the shooter was all about?"

At that, Harley stopped his rage-filled retort, and then

he nodded slowly. "You know it's possible. Because I know for a fact that I'm the instigator who came back into town, but it was the motive for the shooter that I didn't understand. I wondered if it was these dogs, but shooting at Jasmine—or her mother? There was no real reason for that."

"No real reason? You took away a War Dog from one of our *upstanding citizens* who skates the law all the time."

Harley growled. "The shooting was last night, *Chester*. I just got the dogs less than an hour ago. *Today*. The day *after* last night's shooting."

Chester shook his head. "Give me a break here."

"No fucking way. Get your damn head in the game or turn in your badge." Chester remained quiet. At last Harley thought he had the guy's attention. "You are fully aware that your *upstanding citizens* were dealing in drugs and whatever else is going on in the windowless warehouse on the compound. They're not doing *legal* things in secret. They are hiding their illegal activities that you and they both know that they aren't allowed to do. How come I'm here for War Dogs and know more about what's going on in your own town than you do?"

When Chester opened his mouth, Harley raised a hand, shook his head. "Don't. I can hardly stand to look at you, someone Jasmine considers a friend. Anyway, this morning I was supposed to see the guy who sold Bowser to the drug-runners, but, when I went by his place, nobody was home."

Chester got some of his wits about him. "Who's that?"

"Hank Guilford."

At that, Chester winced. "Hank's always in trouble. He's a heavy-duty drunk and a gambler. If he can sell or do anything for money, he will. He got the dog from his father, who up and died of a heart attack not too long ago. He was a good man. The son, not so much."

"Well, that's what happens when he sold a War Dog he wasn't allowed to."

"That sounds like Hank." Chester faced Harley. "Look. I want to do right by Jasmine. And I would appreciate it if you didn't tell her about … earlier."

Harley shook his head. "No. I won't give you any promise at all. That was your one and only slip-up allowed. You understand me?"

Chester stood a little taller. "Noted." Then he seemed to swallow the fear in his throat. "You'll bring charges against him?" He pointed at the downed guy.

"Would it do any good?"

"Maybe not," the deputy admitted. "That kid's on a down … downward loser streak."

"And now the drug boss will know he was sold something he wasn't allowed to buy."

"And that could cause more trouble than I need right now." He glared at Harley, getting his spine back. "You've put us in a hell of a pickle."

"Or you could take this as an opportunity to clean up this very unpleasant element in your town."

"They weren't causing any trouble."

"If you don't think moving millions of dollars of drugs is a problem, what about him trying to go countrywide now? Or did you not know about that either?"

At that, the guy winced. "Surely there's no way he's getting that kind of money in here."

"I don't know whether he's getting drugs out of Canada or if he's moving them into Canada, but it's a perfect storm. The compound property borders right along the edge of two countries. For all you know, there's a damn tunnel going from one side to the other."

"Most of that border is completely unsecured. They wouldn't even have to do that."

"Exactly," Harley noted. "So will you do something about this?"

The guy hesitated.

"I'm just here to tell you that already my bosses know about this and know what's going down, so there could be an awful lot of repercussions."

"Shit," he muttered in disgust. "You leaving any time soon? Don't leave us with another mess."

"The mess was yours," he declared in a hard voice, "including a climate where a girl can't even come to the sheriff and let them know that she's been raped."

"That's an entirely different story. I was only a few years older than her."

"Did you go to that party too?"

He stopped, looked at him. "Which party?"

"Just after I left. It was the first and only one she went to."

"Yeah, I was there." He frowned in confusion. "Are you telling me that's where it happened?"

"Yep, that's exactly where it happened."

He stopped and shook his head. "A lot of people were there."

"Which is why she had a lot of trouble getting anybody to listen to her because, of course, nobody wanted to hear anything—other than I was to blame."

"That was her father." The deputy grew quiet. "He always had it out for you. And you're right—because you left, you made a good scapegoat."

"Except that she knew, and she also knew that, even

though she talked to somebody at the sheriff's office, nobody did anything about it."

"I'll have to look into that." Chester scratched his head. "Because that's not right at all. I knew her well back then. But, once she got pregnant and had to stay home to look after the child, well, she changed."

"You think? Rape will do that to a woman too."

He shook his head. "I had no clue."

"But you were at the party."

"Yeah, but so was everybody else."

"Anything weird happened? Any drugs happening?"

"Lots. Typical teenage party."

"And yet nothing untoward or nothing made you think that something really ugly was going on?"

He shook his head. "I had a girlfriend back then. Honestly, I was only interested in getting laid myself."

"Well, so was somebody else at that same party, and he sure as hell wasn't worried about getting consent for it."

At that, the deputy winced. "Jesus. I'll have to talk to her about that."

"Good luck. She's a little on the bitter side."

"Of course she is."

The guy on the ground started to moan, coming to.

Chester looked down at the guy. "So are you pressing charges against him?"

"Nope. Are you?"

He shook his head. "No."

"In that case, I'll take the dogs, and I'm heading back."

"Back where?" he asked. "You've opened up a war with drug-runners, and that'll just bring a lot of trouble on somebody else's shoulders."

Thinking about that, knowing he would stick around for

a bit, Harley needed new accommodations, someplace with room for two big dogs. "At least I've got what I came for. And don't go blaming me for any of this. Your town always stank. You just didn't want to identify the smell."

CHAPTER 7

THE GOSSIP WAS rampant, as usual. Jasmine heard from several different neighbors about a big conflag in the industrial section of town, involving dogs and Harley. Everybody was talking about how he was trouble right from the get-go. She shook her head at that because she knew that the story was growing proportionately. She had texted Harley a couple times, and, when her phone rang for the umpteenth time, she looked at it to see it was finally him answering. "Are you okay?" she asked.

"I'm okay," he answered in surprise. "Are you? You've left several messages."

"Yes. The town's gossiping about your actions this morning."

"What actions?" he asked curiously.

"About the conflagration in getting the War Dog back."

"Well, Bowser is with me. That's for sure, but there wasn't much of a conflag."

"Well, I'm glad you got him back. What about the guy hanging on to him?"

"I left him unconscious on the street."

"You what?" She gasped in surprise.

"Yeah. Well, he wasn't friendly."

"I can't say that I'm upset," she added. "He threatened me this morning."

"He what?"

At that, she quickly filled him in on the situation. "That was one of the reasons why I contacted you this morning."

"Yeah. I've been crazy busy. I've got two dogs now because I took the other one away as well. And now I'm trying to find a place for them."

"You can bring them here."

"No. I can't do that. You've got your mom and your son there."

"Right, but I have a fenced-in yard as well. I mean, there's no reason that the dogs won't help defend us against whoever that shooter was."

"Well …" He stopped, thinking about it.

"Bring them here."

"I don't know how dangerous they are."

"Why would they be dangerous?"

"Because I don't know what training they've had since they were with the department."

"Do you think the second one was in the department too?"

"I'm not sure. That's still in the realm of 'I've got to sort it out.' I'm at the vet right now with them, getting them checked over."

"Are they okay?"

"Bowser's neck is pretty chewed up from the pronged collar the guy had on him. The asshole had it set that, at any time, with even the lightest of pulls, it would cut through Bowser's skin. Plus he had him wired to a damn shock collar."

"Oh my. Poor dog."

"His life is not what it was originally, but we'll try to make it better now. I just want to make sure no other injuries are on them."

"I still say, bring them here afterward."

"I'll think about it. You'll let me know if that asshole comes back, okay?"

"Oh, I will. that's the last thing I want." She hung up, turned to put on the teakettle, then decided to check on her mom first. She had been knitting quietly this morning. Jasmine didn't know what her mother was working on, but, as long as she was doing something and appeared to be happy, it was all good. "Mom, I'll put on a pot of tea. Do you want a cup?"

Her mother didn't say a word.

She walked closer. "Mom?" But still got no answer. Her mom was knitting away but didn't appear to even hear her. Jasmine sat down beside her. "Hey?"

At that, her mother looked up, looked at her, smiled. "Hi, how nice to see you."

And sadly she realized her mom was off in her other world again. "Would you like a cup of tea?"

"That would be lovely, thank you. I'm waiting for my daughter to come visit."

"I am your daughter, Mom."

"I know you keep saying that." She smiled, while nodding. "It's very nice of you to pretend to be my daughter, but my daughter will be here soon."

"If you say so." She got up, put on the teakettle, and stared out the window, wondering what people did in this situation to handle the heartbreak of watching their parents disappear from them. It was just sad. When the doorbell rang, she walked to the front door to find Chester there. "Hey, did you get any information on the shooter?"

He shook his head. "I talked to Harley this morning.

May I come in?"

Her eyebrows shot up at her friend's tone, now in full deputy mode. She nodded and stepped farther back to let him in. He took a look at her mom. "Hello, Matilda."

Matilda looked up, smiled at him. "Hello there. Did you bring my daughter with you?"

He looked over at Jasmine in confusion.

She shrugged. "She's waiting for her daughter to come visit," she said, as if by an explanation.

He nodded. "Sorry, no." When Matilda dropped her head and went back to her knitting, Jasmine led Chester through to the kitchen. He noted, "She's getting worse, isn't she?"

"She is, indeed. So what did you find out?"

He hesitated. "Well, this is a little awkward right now, but I did talk to Harley this morning."

"Yeah, it's been *great* having Harley back." Her tone was wry. "All kinds of crap's coming out."

"And that's what I want to talk to you about. Everybody assumed that Jimmy was his."

She winced at that. "Everybody assumed that because *that* was easier for everybody to believe than anything else."

"Harley said that you went to a party and was raped."

"And Harley's correct, but I don't appreciate him telling you."

"Maybe not, but it was my fault because I trashed him for leaving you pregnant."

She winced at that. "Yeah, and I can see that he would have a problem with that because it's not who he is."

"You've always believed in him, whereas nobody else was really of the same impression that he was the good guy who you thought he was."

"No, … nobody believed in him but me, which is one of the reasons why I had such a hard time when he left."

"I would have left too," Chester stated. "You were underage, and your dad was a mean son of a bitch."

She looked at him in surprise. "Well, I knew he was. I didn't think anybody else thought that."

"He was cheap. He was vindictive, and he was mean. I'm surprised Harley lasted as long as he did."

"Harley had a goal. He would get through high school and hit the navy." She shrugged. "He made his dreams come true, and, for that, I understand."

"But you expected him to come back for you, didn't you?"

"Not once I got pregnant," she quietly replied. "I figured that I wasn't good enough."

"Ouch. Do you want to tell me what happened that night?"

"You could check the files. I reported it."

He stared at her in shock.

She nodded. "Doesn't mean that my dad didn't do something to squash it though. I always wondered."

"Oh, God." Chester rubbed a hand down his face. "I hope not."

"Well, he wasn't a very nice man in many ways."

"That's beyond not being nice."

"They were all about appearances. Remember?"

He nodded slowly. "I really …" And then he stopped. "I'll have to go back to the files and see if anything's there. I've been a deputy for a decade, and, as far as I know, there's been no hint of anything."

"Well, it happened at the party that you were at."

He looked at her and nodded. "Once Harley told me

about it, I realized I'd been there too," he murmured, "but I didn't see anything like that."

"Well, the drugs were openly there." She stopped for a moment, waited for Chester to respond, then she mentioned a bunch of other students who were there.

He nodded. "I saw them all."

"What about the hard drugs, cocaine and heroin there? Did you see those?"

He shook his head. "Sometimes I wonder if my eyes were even open. After I talked to Harley, it's just like it was a completely different party."

"I'm not so sure about that, as much as you were just very focused on your girlfriend."

"With good reason. I was desperate to get laid."

She burst out laughing. "Well, … I imagine you did. You were working it pretty hard."

He rolled his eyes. "I was a young hormonal teen. Pardon me for trying to make one of the basics in life happen."

"I get it. But I didn't ask for it, and that's what I got too."

"Do you know who did it?"

"No. Absolutely no idea."

"No hints?"

"Well, I was with Perry, Jason, Jackson, Julie. Howrath was there."

"Howrath?"

She nodded. "Yeah. Why?"

"He died that night of the party."

She looked at him in shock. "What are you talking about?"

"You didn't hear?"

"No, I didn't hear anything."

"He was killed in a car accident."

"Well, I knew he died in a car accident." She frowned. "I didn't know it was that night."

"Yep, and he was under the influence of drugs."

"Well, if an investigation was ever done, you can probably take his circle of friends, and it was one of them who was at the party." She hesitated. "And the guy Harley knocked out today was the one who threatened me this morning."

He stared at her in shock. "Whoa. He didn't even tell me about that."

"No, it just happened this morning. I took pictures of the guy with Bowser, the War Dog. Here I'll send them to you now." She brought up her phone and sent the pictures. Chester brought them up on his phone and flicked through them. "Also this same guy also gloated that he knew what happened to me that night." She stared at him as he studied the face.

"Jesus." Chester's gaze widened as he looked from his phone to her. "Seriously?"

"With a gun in his hand too, yeah." She gave him what she remembered of the conversation.

"Maybe I need to go pick him up and have a talk with him."

"I'd like it if you did. Now that I've got Harley here"—she shook her head—"a whole lot of things are coming out in a very different way."

"Yeah, ya think?" He shook his head. "That's a scary thought though that you were threatened. I'll go talk to him and see what he's got to say for himself."

"I'm sure he'll say I lied completely," she murmured.

"He wasn't there that night of the party, was he?"

"Who? Him? I don't even know this asshole who was at

my house this morning."

He stopped and looked at her. "If it's the same one I'm thinking of, the guy Harley knocked out this morning, that was Jackson."

"Julie's boyfriend?"

"Yeah."

"I didn't recognize him." She thought about it, then added, "Jackson was definitely there at the party. He was handing out drugs to most of the people. An awful lot of colored pills were passed around."

"Jesus." Chester stared off into space. "However, date-rape drugs are liquid."

"Yeah, well, remember the punch?"

"So you think somebody spiked your glass?"

"I think it's the only thing that could have happened. I wasn't drinking anything but the punch."

"That punch was already laced with enough alcohol to knock everybody out," he reminded her.

"I know." She paused. "It was a bit of a shock when I had my first sip, but you know I had some, and I nursed that glass a lot. I was smarting from the fact that Harley had left, and I was looking to have a good time," she noted sarcastically. "What I ended up with was a whole different story."

"I'll get back to you." He walked toward the front door.

"You do that." She grimaced. "Keep it on the down-low, please. There's still an innocent victim in all of this, and that's my son."

"HERE'S THE RECEIPT." The vet's receptionist handed it to Harley.

Harley glanced at it, before folding it and putting it in his wallet. "I'm glad it's not worse."

"The one dog's malnourished, and she's got a broken rib. Bowser, however, has quite a few lacerations around his neck and lower area. He's also been wearing a chain around his chest, which a lot of guys use to control the animal so they can't breathe."

"How does that do anything good?" Harley asked in an anguished voice.

"No good at all. So, we've got antibiotics here for Bowser, and you've got a solution here to clean the cuts and an ointment to help those wounds heal." She handed over the bottles.

He nodded and looked down at the two dogs. "I only have a leash for the one."

"We've got a rope for you, unless you want to buy a collar." She pointed to the store side of the clinic.

He walked over and picked up one, tried it on the female. She whined but didn't resist. He nodded. "This one's good and won't be too tight." And he picked up a lead for her too and quickly paid for both. With both dogs, he walked back out to the truck. This rental had a double cab with a back seat too, and he didn't want to put them in the truck bed, and he surely didn't want to cause any further conflict over these dogs with the drug-running crowd or even the townsfolk here. Neither did he know quite what he would do as far as housing the dogs now, especially since Harley wasn't ready to leave yet. Not with things stirring up against Jasmine—a gunshot into her home, threats on her life, then taunts of what happened at the party long ago.

Harley picked up the phone and called Daniel.

"You're causing trouble already, aren't you?" Daniel

asked, not really expecting an answer.

"Apparently." Harley's voice was harsh. "I found the War Dog being badly treated. So I've reclaimed him and the other one that they had."

"Lots of guys won't take that very kindly."

"Well, the vet's checked both for microchips. When I get a chance, I'll check with the military War Dog database to see if both of them are ours. They've got similar training but that doesn't make them official. Lots of that training is public now."

"Could be any kind of a dog. The guys at the compound really pride themselves on their dogs out there."

"Maybe. A couple other things have been happening here too."

"What's that?"

"Well, for one, somebody shot through the kitchen window at Jasmine's. I have to fix that window, but then we've got to find that shooter."

"What?"

"Yeah. Her mom was in the kitchen making lemonade, and somebody fired through the window. Her mom's okay. Shattered the glass and scared Jasmine pretty badly."

"Ya think?" Daniel snorted. "Jesus Christ, what's going on?"

Harley hesitated. "It's not really my story, yet it is now. You're the one who told me about her child, and I already told you that I wasn't the father, but she finally confessed to me that she went to a party the weekend after I left …" He let his voice trail off, knowing that she wouldn't appreciate it if he told everybody.

"Yeah, I was there. Most of the town was there."

"Well, somebody gave her a date-rape drug, raped her

that night, and, when she woke up the next morning, she tried to tell her parents and the sheriff, and nobody would listen."

Daniel's voice was shocked. "Jesus Christ! Are you serious?"

"Very serious. She doesn't even know who the father is. The morning after, she did have the wherewithal to take some pictures of the condition she was in and left those with the sheriff. I talked with Chester this morning too because he came upon me, after I just had the issue with the dog handlers." Harley then told his friend what the one handler had said to Jasmine—after threatening her at her own home with a gun. "I'd like to know who it was because you haven't seen me mad yet. And it'll be hell to pay when I do find out. I can't believe he did that to her."

"Got it. Not just you though. Another girl I know of had a bad time that night. She didn't want to tell me anything about it back then."

"Another girl?"

"Yeah, Cindy. She moved away a couple years afterward. She said that the party had been a really bad experience for her. I didn't know what she meant because I was having a grand old time, but she didn't really follow up and wouldn't talk to me about it."

"Now you probably have a good idea what happened. Your nice little town has got a really dark underbelly."

"I still can't believe it. Jesus, what Jasmine went through ..."

"And then her father wouldn't let her do anything about it. But, of course, her parents held it over her for life. Including taking half of her babysitting money that she earned, looking after kids while raising her son."

"Yeah, her dad was a real mean piece of shit. I'm not at all unhappy he's gone."

"Maybe not, but she's had the aftermath the whole time. I'm back. We're clearing the air."

"Is that why you think she was shot at through the window?"

"I don't know, but when I asked her what else had changed in her world, she mentioned the only thing was my return. And I didn't figure out what the hell that meant, until she told me what had happened when I was gone. And I figure either that the rapist knows that I'm back—and he's afraid of getting found out—or that something else is going on. I just can't imagine what—but you can bet I'll find out."

"Look. If you need any help," Daniel said, "call me."

"I've got two massive dogs to look after right now, and you're not set up for animals. Do you have any recommendation of another hotel I can go to?"

"Jesus, I'll have to think about that. Nothing's even here in town. It's just us."

"Jasmine suggests they go to her place because she has a fenced backyard."

"It's not the worst idea in the world. However, you might be bringing trouble her way, but you could be anyway. At least you'd be on spot to look after her, should something go down over this. Besides, those dogs need care, and she's pretty good with them."

"Maybe. I'll think about it." And, with that, Harley hung up.

CHAPTER 8

JASMINE LOOKED OVER at her son. "Would you mind if Harley stayed with us for a few days?"

Jimmy looked at her, surprised, and then a calculating look entered his gaze. "Is he your boyfriend?"

"No." She shook her head. "He was years ago, yes, when I was young, too young," she admitted. "But he is a friend, and he's back in town, and he has two dogs that he needs a place to keep safe. We have a fenced-in backyard."

"Wow." Jimmy stared at her. "You've always refused to let me have a dog, and now this guy pops back into your life, and you'll let him bring two?"

He sounded both irritated and awestruck that dogs could be coming. She smiled at him. "Circumstances are obviously very different."

"Somewhat, but I don't know about how much."

"So what's your answer?" she asked him.

"Why are you asking me though? Because it's your house. It's your home. And, as much as I might want to have a dog, and you've always said no. Apparently this guy has some sway over you."

"While I would have loved to give you a dog, I didn't want one for many reasons."

"Like what?" Jimmy asked. When she hesitated, he added, "I really want to know."

"First, no matter all your good intentions, taking care of any dog would end up being my responsibility to feed, to water, to wash, to clean up after. I'm already taking care of Mom and the house and you. I think that's enough on my plate." She held up her hand before he argued with her. "I know that, as you get older, you'll help more. Still, it falls mostly to me. Second, we don't need any added expenses here. So, with Harley's dogs, he takes care of them, and he pays for their food. And it's only temporary too." She added patiently, "Harley's a good man. The dogs were in trouble, so he rescued them, and he's trying to find a hotel where they can be with him, until he finds a more permanent solution."

"What kind of trouble?"

"That's for him to tell you. One of them is a War Dog that he came here to find."

Jimmy looked at her in surprise, and his eyes lit up. "Like one of those that go to war with all that training to help out the soldiers?"

"Yes." She nodded. "And the dog is retired after so many years and was adopted out, then somehow ended up with some other guy who turned around and sold him to these people who were abusing the dog."

"That's not fair," Jimmy noted.

"No, it sure isn't." She smiled. "The thing is, Harley currently has two large dogs, saving them both from abuse. They were both in rough shape, but one definitely had more injuries from the mistreatment that they had received. So Harley's trying to find a pet-friendly hotel. But, if he doesn't, then he needs a place to bring them."

"Of course he can come here. You know how I feel about dogs, and, why anybody would want to hurt them, I don't know."

"Because people sometimes aren't the best that they can be."

He snorted at that. "You always say things in such a nice way, Mom. Why don't you just be honest and say people are assholes?"

"Stop," she said immediately. "We don't use that language here."

He rolled his eyes at her, got up, and opened the fridge. "When's dinner?"

"Do you ever do anything but eat?" she asked.

"I would, but that hunger usually stops me." He gave her a cheeky grin. "What are we having anyway?"

"There'll be burgers."

"Oh, good." He stopped, looked at her. "Did you invite him too?"

"I did, but I haven't heard whether he's coming or not."

"Why wouldn't he tell you?"

"Because of the dogs, remember? He's at the vet's right now."

At that, her son's smile dropped away. "They're really hurt, aren't they?"

"One is more so than the other, yes, but they'll both live."

"Good. I'm glad he rescued them. That's just wrong to harm dogs like that, especially hero dogs."

"It is. But it doesn't stop the abuse just because we want it to stop."

He nodded. "I can't wait very long to eat. Why don't you text him and see how much longer until he'll be here."

"I think he doesn't want to come here with the dogs. So I'm sure he's intent on looking for a hotel."

"Tell him to come here anyway. That's just foolish. Why go to a hotel if we have a fenced-in yard?" He turned, looked at the busted window. "You didn't get that fixed yet either, did you?"

"No, but Harley said he'll board it up. And I have somebody coming out tomorrow morning to give us an estimate on the replacement cost."

"Right, but do you have the money for it?"

"I don't know." She shrugged. "Not really. But we'll make do."

"Well, Grandma does."

"Grandma's money, yes, and it is Grandma's house, yes, and we do have to get stuff fixed, but you know how I feel about using her money. Still, we *are* fixing her house."

"Don't have a lot of choices, when it's also her house, and you're her caregiver."

"I know that." Jasmine gave a tired sigh because they'd had this argument a lot. "And like I've told you before, that money usually goes to looking after us. It won't cover a window and our living expenses too."

"You're her full-time caregiver, twenty-four hours a day. You sure there isn't enough money for somebody else to do that?"

"There isn't enough money for me to pay somebody else to take care of Grandma, no." She bowed her head and grimaced. "Absolutely, I know that."

"Of course, and that just proves that you don't get paid enough money yourself for taking care of Grandma."

"I've been trying to save a little bit, trying to get ahead of things." She looked at the window and sighed. "But I may have to use that for the window."

"I wouldn't worry about it. You need to get it fixed regardless." He bolted to his feet. "If burgers aren't for a while, can I go over to Terry's place?" And, with that, Jimmy was already at the front door.

"But you have to be back in an hour."

"What? Why an hour?"

"Remember that part about burgers?"

"Okay." With a nod, he disappeared.

At least food was a motivator for him. She listened to her son bolt out the door and run down the steps out front. He was a good kid, even if he didn't always understand. She had to remember that, for all his maturity, the kid was only eleven. She also had a hard time taking the money that she needed for her care—never about Jimmy's though, except on a severely restricted budget. That mind-set of hers was just part and parcel of having lived here with her parents—all the time knowing that she hadn't been welcome to stay, had it not been for birthing a boy.

And Jasmine, while sharing food and shelter with her parents, had never been given any money by them—instead giving her money to them. But now that she was looking after her mom, it was one of those hard decisions about how much was enough, whether about money for her and Jimmy or about Jasmine taking on her mother's declining mental health.

The government did give Jasmine a certain amount of money for being a full-time caregiver, but her mother had also made it very clear that Jasmine had to pay rent regardless. So it was a back-and-forth situation, but now Mom wasn't fully functioning and didn't know whether Jasmine paid rent or not—but Jasmine herself knew. And that meant that she couldn't allow herself to take advantage. And it felt like she was taking advantage. The mental strain was enormous.

She groaned as she stared out the window. "When will this ever end?" she muttered to herself. Because, of course, it wouldn't end, as her mother was still in good physical health. At that, Jasmine got up, walked out to the living room to check on her mom, sitting with her hands folded in her lap, staring blankly out the window.

"Mom?" Her mother didn't even move. Jasmine sat down beside her, right in her line of sight, so she was blocking any view out the window, but her mother didn't react at all. "Mommy, you okay?"

When she got no answer, Jasmine groaned and sat back. "We go from one good day to half of a good day to half of a morning. That's good too. Even an hour's good," she reminded herself, then shook her head. "These sessions are getting worse."

She didn't know what to do. Her mother had a doctor's appointment tomorrow, and Jasmine would see just what the doctor recommended at that point. She wasn't sure anybody could do anything, honestly. It seemed like her mom's decline had increased so fast. Jasmine slumped, filled with worry—more worries—when her phone rang.

She looked at the screen and saw it was Harley. "Hey." She stood, shifting gears. "How'd your day go?"

"I can't find a hotel that's got any room for me to bring the dogs," he said in frustration.

"And I told you that you could bring them here. And honestly, Jimmy is delighted at the idea."

Harley stopped for a moment. "Are you sure? I hate to even bother you, but I do need a place."

"Then come. Burgers are planned for another forty-five minutes from now."

"I can bring groceries."

"Not today but you will need to bring something for the dogs."

"Right. I'll take a look through the pet store and pick up something."

"Good idea." She hung up and walked into the kitchen. She opened the fridge to make sure she had enough burgers thawing to include Harley. If he ate anything like her son, she wouldn't eat tonight at all. She pulled out another package of hamburger and carefully defrosted it in the microwave, taking her time to do it on low temp for a little bit and then turning it. She hated it when it dried out and cooked on one side and was raw on the other.

With it thawed, she put it into the bowl, with the rest of the meat, and quickly mixed in the spices. By the time she was done, she heard a vehicle outside. She washed her hands and stepped onto the front porch. Sure enough, it was Harley.

He hopped out, and she watched him get into the passenger side and stood there, doing something. She saw dogs on the inside but not enough to understand what Harley was doing. He slowly let one out, and the dog had bandages on its neck and another one on its side. A cone was around its neck, and the dog didn't look at all impressed.

Jasmine walked down the steps to the sidewalk, heading toward the little gate to the backyard. "Wow, he doesn't look very happy."

"Dogs don't like the cones."

She looked at the second dog, who didn't have a cone. "That one looks to be in better shape."

"She is, at that, but they're both nervous and high-strung." Harley walked them over and held out the less injured one and introduced her to Jasmine. "I'm not sure what name this one goes by, but I'm calling her Queen."

Jasmine reached down and held out her hand. Queen sniffed and gave her a little bit of a tail wag, but her gaze was interested in the surrounding area. "She looks pretty interested in what's going on."

"And with good reason. I think they're also probably hungry."

He pulled the second dog forward. "And this one, with the cone over his head, this is the one I've been looking for. This is Bowser."

"Hello, Bowser," she said in a gentle voice. "How are you, boy?" He gave her a tail wag and leaned into her. "So is he leaning into me because he wants cuddles or because he's hoping I'll take this thing off his neck?"

"Both." Harley laughed. She scratched him gently on the cheek. "Avoid his neck though," he warned. "Lots of stitches and sore spots. We've got antibiotics for both of them."

"I feel so bad." She stood, shaking her head. "How could anybody even begin to hurt these animals?"

"Bad people find it easy to hurt them. And it's just wrong, but it won't necessarily change anytime soon."

"And that's just wrong too."

With both the dogs inside the small fenced yard and getting used to the place, she led the way to the kitchen. "I feel like they'll have to be on a leash the whole time." She suddenly worried about how her mother would handle them.

"It's hard to say. War Dogs are highly trained. We'll see. Once we get them fed, I'll check the fence and see if I need to do anything further to secure them here." He shrugged. "We might just leave them out here. Still, we need to introduce the dogs to your mom, so the dogs know she is a friend."

"That could work." Jasmine was a little relieved. As they all came into the house, the dogs on leashes, Jasmine called out, "Mom, we're here, and Harley has two dogs with him."

But her mother just stared vacantly at the window.

Jasmine sighed. "She's been like this most of the afternoon. Earlier today she seemed really happy and normal, but she quickly went downhill again."

"I imagine every day is a challenge for her now."

"Absolutely." She walked into the kitchen, thankful the dogs hadn't barked or reacted negatively to her mom. "Let's get them outside right now." And she carried on through to the backyard. With the glass sliding doors at the rear of the house opened, the two dogs came outside, sniffing, and one rolled on the ground and just laid there.

"That didn't seem to go too badly." She laughed. "He seems to be happy to be back here."

"And with good reason. I also have food." He looked at her hesitantly. "Are you okay to handle the leashes while I go get the bag of food?"

She nodded and took them from him ever-so-gingerly. "I just don't have much experience with big dogs."

"I don't think you have to do anything. I'll be right back."

As he turned to back away, the dogs watched him with intent gazes.

"They don't look like they want you leaving."

"It's okay. I'll be right back."

And she sat down at a little nearby table, holding both leashes, as both dogs stood and waited, their gazes on the door that Harley had disappeared into.

"He'll be back," she reassured them. They flicked their

gazes her way and then back to the door. And she just sat here and waited. Harley returned within minutes, with a big bag of dog food and a couple bowls. They looked at him, with more interest directed at the dog food, and then she handed over the leashes. "I'll form the burgers, while you look after them."

He nodded. "Not a problem. I'll feed them right here, if you don't mind."

She looked around, nodded. "Maybe off at the corner over there, where nobody will accidentally interrupt them. I don't know what they're like when they've got food, but I would hate for anybody—like my mother and my son—to come out here and disturb them in any way and get a little more reaction than they thought."

"Good point." Harley moved the bowls off to the side, then, using a pocketknife he pulled from his pocket, he quickly cut open the bag and scooped each bowl in, filling it full. Then he set them both down, looked at her, intently watching the interaction. "Do you happen to have one big bowl for water?" She nodded and hurried inside. She returned in a minute with a bowl and handed it to him. "There's also a tap on the corner there."

He nodded, filled the bowl with fresh water, and put it between the two bowls of food. Then both dogs walked closer to the food. The one that wasn't hurt as badly had immediately shoved her face into the bowl and started to eat. But Bowser just sat here and looked at Harley.

He told Bowser, "It's okay, boy. You can eat."

But he laid down, obviously not happy or not hungry or still feeling the effects from the stitches and the antibiotics. Harley walked over and sat down beside him.

"Not doing too good today, are you, buddy?" The dog's

tail wagged, happily grateful to have some attention that wasn't mean. As Harley carefully scratched the dog, Bowser leaned into him, until he was stretched across his lap. Harley spent a long time just cuddling the dogs, especially after the second one had eaten.

"We'll call you Bowser and Queen," he said. "We can't be giving you a boy's name now, can we, Queenie?"

With that, the dogs barked and cuddled up closer.

Jasmine had been standing in the doorway, watching for the longest time. He looked over at her and smiled. "See? They are good dogs, despite being mistreated by bad people."

"I just wanted to know for sure."

"I wouldn't have brought them here if I had thought they were dangerous to you or your family."

"I appreciate that, but, at the same time, I also have to look after my family and need to know for sure that it's okay in my own heart."

"Understood. You okay now?"

"I'm fine. Do you think they've had enough to eat?"

"Queen has. I may need to wet Bowser's food for him. As long as the bowl's there, and they know they can come back and forth and eat at will, I don't think it would be an issue."

She nodded. "Now I'll go get those burgers made up."

He grinned. "Do I get two?"

"Is two enough?" she asked seriously.

"Yes, how many does Jimmy eat?"

"Two or three. I just wasn't sure how many I needed to fix for you."

"Two's fine."

She nodded and went back in and quickly formed the

patties. When she came back outside, he asked, "Where is your son?"

"Over at his friend's." She looked at the barbecue and then pulled out her phone. "I'll tell him to get his butt home. I don't want to start the barbecue before I know when he'll be back for sure." She dialed her son's number, and, when he didn't answer, she groaned and then phoned his friend's house. "Can you send Jimmy back home, please?" she said. "Burgers are going on soon."

"Jimmy's not here." Wendy laughed. "You lose him again?"

"Oh," she whispered in frustration. "Is your son there?"

"Yeah, he was expecting Jimmy to come over, but he didn't, so we figured that he went somewhere else."

"He wasn't supposed to." Jasmine sighed. "Thanks, I'll track him down."

"You do that."

She hung up the phone, turned toward Harley, who was already on his feet, staring at her with a look of concern on his face. "Is this something that you should worry about?"

"Normally, no, but right now? After the threats? I don't know."

"Where's the house Jimmy should have been at?" She quickly pointed out four houses down. "So he would have gone from your house to that house?"

"And normally that would not be a big deal." She bit her bottom lip.

"We'll go take a look." And bringing the dogs with him, Harley quickly checked their leashes to make sure they were secured. "We'll go out at the side gate."

She nodded, and, still chewing her bottom lip, she watched as Harley led both dogs around the side and out to the front yard. She covered up the raw burgers on the kitchen counter, quickly washed her hands, grabbed her sweater, and stepped out on the front porch steps. She watched as Harley walked down the sidewalk with the dogs at his side. She didn't know if they were dogs that could track, but, even if they were, they didn't have anything with Jimmy's scent on it.

Harley stopped two houses down to talk to one of the neighbors. The neighbor pointed out down the street toward her house. Harley nodded, and he came back at a quick pace. "Your neighbor saw him get into a truck."

She stared at him, shaking her head. "Jimmy knows better than to get into a vehicle."

"Can we presume then that maybe he knew them?"

"I don't care if they knew him or not," she said, her voice rising. "He knows better." She walked down to the neighbor and saw the older guy toddling toward her. "Hey, Tom. Did you recognize the vehicle?"

"Just an old beat-up white truck. Jimmy seemed to be comfortable with it though."

"He never jumps into a vehicle like that. He's supposed to let me know if his plans change. Do you think he knew the driver?"

"No clue."

He told them that they headed off down that direction though, and the old guy pointed down the street.

"I guess you didn't catch the license plate, did you?" Harley asked.

He shook his head immediately. "No, I didn't think anything was wrong."

"And there may not be," Harley replied immediately. "Just because he got into a vehicle doesn't mean that it's an emergency."

"That's right." Tom nodded. "That's right. He's a sensible young man. He knows better than to worry his mama like that."

"Yeah, he does," she agreed, her voice getting hard. "I'll have a talking to with him when he gets home."

She raced back up to the house, calling Jimmy on her phone as she walked. Again there was no answer; she contacted her deputy friend, Chester. "Jimmy got into a vehicle—an old beat-up white truck—without letting me know. He was due home about twenty minutes ago. I have no idea where he is, and he's not answering his phone."

"And you think something's wrong?"

"Yes, of course, I think something's wrong," she snapped. "I just wondered if you know anything about a white pickup that's troublesome."

"No, not really," he said slowly. "Is Harley there?"

"Yeah, I left him outside with the dogs, checking out the area."

"Good. That might be our best chance, if those dogs find anything."

"Yeah, but one's injured. He's got a big cone on his neck. The other one is in better shape. I don't know what kind of training these dogs have. Besides, they don't know Jimmy's scent at all."

"I know. I know. Look. I'm off shift right now. Let me come by. I'll be there in twenty." And he hung up on her.

She walked back toward Harley and told him.

He nodded. "Give me a piece of Jimmy's clothing that he's worn recently, will you?"

"Will they track?"

"I have no idea. Just because we want them to be trackers doesn't make them trackers either." She quickly raced back inside and grabbed his discarded sweater, brought it outside, and Harley held it to the dogs' noses. One of them started to wag, the female, and she'd immediately barked. "Fine, girl. Let's go search for him."

Her nose dropped to the ground, and she took Harley back to the spot in the road, where Jimmy had gotten into the vehicle. "Well, that confirms what Tom said, but it's obviously of no help past that." Harley looked around. "Street cameras." Harley shook his head. "Small town. No street cameras."

He pulled out his phone and called Badger. "We've got a situation right now. We don't know how critical this is, but young Jimmy isn't answering his phone, and, given everything else that's happening right now, we don't want to take a chance." He quickly filled Badger in.

Badger agreed. "I can take a look and see if we can find anything on satellite. No cameras around? No security cams from neighbors? Nothing like that?"

"No, the deputy is coming around here soon, and we're hoping that maybe they have something, but he didn't even seem to recognize the vehicle."

"And who is it you think has him?"

"I don't know, but she was threatened this morning, her and her family. So, at this point, I'm taking it as a credible threat."

"Definitely. And we're talking about the dog's owner again? Jackson?"

"Yes. I'm wondering about heading back to that warehouse property."

"But you have no right to get onto the actual property itself."

"Nope, and the sheriff doesn't appear to be too bothered about the property either. Although Chester mentioned something about building a case on the compound, it didn't seem too urgent."

"I spoke to somebody else with connections in Eureka, with suspicions as to the drug-runners. They were getting a team together to take a closer look at the warehouse."

"But can they without permission?"

"They've had their eye on the warehouse for a while. If they have a credible lead that something is going on, then definitely. So you forget about that warehouse property, if they can handle that."

"Sure, but I want to know what's on the other property, the compound at the border."

"That reminds me. I meant to contact somebody about that. An RCMP officer I know. See what the status is on that property on the other side."

"Good enough." Harley hung up the phone, faced her, and shrugged. "The warehouse property that the dogs were guarding was under investigation anyway. Some local authorities are getting a team together to go take a look at it."

"And you think they've taken my son?" she asked, barely keeping the horror out of her voice.

"Considering the threat they made to you this morning, I won't disregard the possibility of them doing just that."

"Why would they take him?" She wrapped her arms around her chest, staring at Harley.

"Because it's good leverage," he murmured.

"LEVERAGE?" JASMINE ASKED in a faint voice.

"Yes. Whether it's the dogs they want back or something else, it's leverage. What I don't know is how any of this plays into the shooting into your window."

"And what if it doesn't play in at all?"

"Well, that would be an awful lot of coincidences in your life, all at the same time, after a lifetime of nothing. So then I don't buy that."

"The only thing that's changed," she repeated, "is you."

"Right, and, since I've come here, I've taken the dogs away, dropped their guys on the road, potentially had one quit, and that's only been in what? Twenty-four hours?" he said, with a note of humor.

"It's not funny," she snapped.

He looked at her, nodded, his smile dropping. "You're right. I'll head over there to the warehouse right now and see if I can find your son."

And, with that, he left with the dogs, all headed to the truck. She didn't try to stop him but bounced from leg to leg nervously. He stopped, turned, and looked at her. "You know that I won't let anything happen to him if I can stop it."

"Maybe, but maybe it's already too late."

"That's a pretty high-stakes game for them right now. I highly doubt they'll do anything to hurt him."

"But you can't be sure."

"No, I can't be sure. However, at least take note of the fact that, if it's leverage they want, a dead body is of no value to them."

She closed her eyes, and he watched the color leach from her face. He put the dogs into the back seat of the truck, then walked back over to Jasmine. He leaned down and kissed her gently on the temple. "Let me go see if I can rescue your son," he murmured.

She shook her head. "Jesus, please bring him back alive."

"And you monitor everything going on here. There's a good chance your son'll come bouncing back in, wondering what the stink was about."

"And I'll tan his butt," she said immediately.

He burst out laughing. "I don't think so. You'll be too happy to see him again." He hopped back into the truck and drove down the street. He only had the old white truck to go by. But he knew somebody else who would know an awful lot of locals. He quickly phoned Daniel. "Hey, it looks like Jimmy, Jasmine's son, got into a pickup, an old rattletrap white pickup. We haven't seen hide nor hair of him since, and he's not answering his phone, and he should have been home over an hour ago."

"Jesus. You're rattling things around town, aren't you?"

"The question is, do you have any idea who's got the truck and who might be driving such a vehicle?"

"Lots of old white trucks around here."

"And I don't have a license plate, but the neighbor saw the truck and saw Jimmy get in."

"Interesting," he murmured. "But I can't at the moment pin anything down. I'll think about it though."

"Think fast."

"Will do." And he hung up.

Harley kept driving toward the warehouse property, where he'd taken over the dogs, when Daniel called him back. "I hate to say it, but I think it's one of the drug-runner guys. One of the guys there that handles the dogs has a white truck."

"That's what I was afraid you would say."

"I don't have any way to prove it's him though," Daniel murmured.

"No, I understand that. However, I hear that the Eureka authorities are after that warehouse property, where I reclaimed the dogs today—the same warehouse that they were guarding. And I don't think anybody at the compound knows about it yet, but I need to make sure that Jimmy's not caught up in that too."

"You'll get there first?"

"I'm heading that way. I've got the dogs with me. Just don't know yet if they'll be a help or a hindrance."

"Do you want a hand?"

"If you were single, I'd say, yes, but not now when you've got a pregnant wife and two kids. If I run into trouble, I'll let you know, and maybe then you've got a line for a couple buddies to come down and get me. Otherwise all I could do is just call the sheriff and take my chances."

"They're pretty slow around here."

"So I've heard. I'm sure I'll be fine."

"I'm not so sure you'll be fine," he replied roughly. "Jesus Christ, you come into town, get your head into all kinds of shit, and cause her all kinds of trouble, and that kid goes missing. That's not crap that anybody can deal with alone."

"At least now I'm not alone at this point. I've got at least one War Dog, and I highly suspect that this second one here is too. Honest to God, I'll take them looking after my back before a lot of other people."

"But you don't know that they'll look after your back. They've had a rough couple months, if not a rough couple years. You can't count on their training holding. They are still animals. Their loyalty has to be conflicted."

"I know." Harley looked down at them to see both dogs

placidly staring back at him. But something in their gazes he knew well, and it was called loyalty. "I also saved them from a rough life. And, although it hasn't been very long, and we haven't had a chance to do much bonding, I would still trust them over an awful lot of other people."

"I get it," Daniel agreed. "But please don't do anything stupid. You've got a phone. Use it when you need it. Call in the military. Call in your navy friends. Call in the authorities. Call them all in. You know that girl's been waiting for you to come back for a hell of a long time. Don't make her wish she'd never seen you again because this time you came back, only to die on her." And, with that, Daniel hung up.

Staring at the phone in surprise, Harley thought about it, as he kept on driving. Had Jasmine been waiting for him all this time? If she had, that just made him feel even worse. Sure, she'd had her son in the meantime and was looking after her mother, but was Jasmine really, in the back of her mind, waiting?

He winced and looked at his phone, wondering if he dared pick it up and call her and ask her. Or call Daniel back and get clarification on whether that's really what he meant. Then Harley realized it was something that he needed to have a conversation with her in person. It's not that he hadn't reminded himself over the years to come back. He'd just not given himself an opportunity to even consider following through on those thoughts.

Too much time had passed.

Besides, even if he'd come and had taken a look quietly, he would have seen her with a child, and he'd have immediately assumed that she'd moved on. Even now, knowing the whole story, that was something that would take a little bit of time to adjust to. She had a lot of responsibilities here; it's not like she would just up and move to be with him. Although Harley's life was also on a cusp, so he wasn't sure where he wanted to be either.

CHAPTER 9

JASMINE WAITED AS long as she could before sending him a text twenty minutes after he'd left. **Any news?**

When he came back with **No, not yet**, she sat down at the chair beside her mother, focusing on deep breathing.

Which had her mother looking at her. "If you're feeling ill, you should go to the doctor."

"I'm fine," she murmured, then looked over at her. "Are you okay?"

"Of course I'm fine," she said, with a dismissive wave of her hand. "I'm a Willoughby. We're always fine."

"Even if you're not fine, right?"

"Even then." She nodded. "Did everything I could when I got pregnant. My husband was bound and determined that it would be a boy. I ended up with a girl, and he was not impressed. We tried for years to have a boy, but I never could quite get there."

"I'm sorry," Jasmine replied. "I didn't realize you wanted a son so badly."

"To my husband, only sons were allowed in his world. I mean, I was perfectly happy with the daughter, but he wasn't."

"No, I can see that." Jasmine winced. Her mother didn't realize who she was talking to and was just lost in her memories. "It's too bad he never found a way to love her."

"Well, she was a girl—which, you know, in his mind, wasn't of any value—and, of course, she proved him right by getting pregnant out of a wedlock years later. He was so horrified and completely lost all respect for her."

Jasmine sat here, her heart stuck in her throat, wishing she hadn't brought up the conversation in the first place. She didn't want to hear this. "What about you?" she asked, even though she didn't want to hear the answer.

"Obviously she should have done more to keep her legs closed, but what do you expect when you have a wild child?"

"Was she really wild?" Jasmine asked in a small voice.

"Why she kept on with that useless boy we were forced to keep is beyond me."

"You mean, Harley?"

"Yes, look at his name. Even sounds like he's a bad boy to begin with. We would have never even considered that our daughter would hook up with him. But she did, and that was the result."

"I'm pretty sure your daughter told you that she was raped."

"Of course she'd say that," her mother said, once again with that dismissive wave of her hand. "I mean, she's got to say something, doesn't she? But we never believed her."

After that, her mother fell silent, as Jasmine sat here and stared at the woman she didn't know well and wished that she didn't know as well as she did. Her heart was breaking, as she thought about what her life had been like, when both of her parents had been alive, and how absolutely unloved she'd been all that time.

And how sad for both of them.

They'd had a beautiful, healthy child, and, instead of appreciating what they had, all they wanted was something different. And, even when they got a male foster child, they couldn't see their way to finding any love for him either. She shook her head at that. "You are obviously not a very nice person."

"Nice is for idiots," her mother murmured. "We were successful. That was more important."

"How were you successful?" she asked. "You have no money. Your husband died, leaving you no money."

"Sure, but we raised a family properly. Everybody appreciated the fact that we had done our job right. They looked up to us. My husband was well respected. Success comes in many different forms, and nobody knew that we didn't have any money," she snapped, glaring at Jasmine. "That's very wrong of you to say such a thing."

She shook her head. "I see. So it was all about keeping up appearances."

"That's all there is. What else is there?" And such a bewildered look was on her face that Jasmine knew there was no making sense of it for her mother.

"I guess for you," she said gently, "there wasn't anything."

"Nope, there sure wasn't."

"Where's your daughter now?"

"Off chasing some other boy, I'm sure." She snorted. "Completely useless. She never did get an education or a decent job, and, of course, after she ruined herself, there was no decent marriage in her future. However, that's her problem, not mine."

And, with that, her mother fell silent again.

Feeling nauseated, Jasmine slowly got to her feet and walked into the kitchen. Dry-eyed, she stared out the window that had been shot. She considered how all this was getting worse, what with her son missing, and yet she was still supposed to look after her heartless mother, while Jasmine's heart broke on so many levels. She knew a lot of people would tell her to just ditch the old bat and let the government take care of her.

But Jasmine didn't know how to even do that because of the guilt inside her. She wanted to believe that, somewhere along the line, her mother had loved her. She had to believe that; otherwise everything in her world was a lie.

As she stared down at her trembling hands, she figured it was already a lie. She just wasn't ready to acknowledge the full truth, and how sad was that. She took several slow deep breaths, as she waited for her heart to calm down. When her mother cried out, Jasmine raced back into the living room to see she'd fallen. Jasmine crouched beside her mom. "Are you okay?"

Her mother looked up at her, dazed. "I fell," she moaned. "I was trying to get up, and my hip gave out." She tried to roll over and let out a screech of pain.

Realizing that the fall was likely to be a little more than she had initially thought, Jasmine checked her over, and, as soon as her hands got anywhere close to her mother's hip, her mother cried out in pain. Jasmine immediately called 9-1-1 for an ambulance. As soon as she did that, she grabbed a blanket to cover her mom and sat beside her. "Hold on. An ambulance is coming."

Her mother started to cry louder and louder. "It hurts. It hurts. *It hurts.*"

Nothing Jasmine could do would make it any easier, and, with relief, she heard the sirens outside. She dashed to the front door and let in the paramedics. They took one look, and immediately an EMT went back for a gurney.

Even as the one guy carefully positioned her mom's hip for ease of transport, her mother was crying terribly. Jasmine looked at the two EMTs. "I presume she's broken a hip?"

"Definitely looks like it. But we'll know more, as soon as we get her checked out at the hospital. Are you coming right now?"

Jasmine stopped and then looked at him. "My son's gone missing. Everybody's out looking for him." They looked at her in shock. She nodded, wrapped her arms around herself. "Take her to the hospital. I'll be there as soon as I can."

They nodded, loaded her mom into the ambulance, and took her away.

Jasmine stood on the front porch, feeling the guilt claw away at her throat. She could have gone with her mom, except that she should remain here, waiting for her son to come home. She closed her eyes and whispered, "Please, Jimmy. Please come home now."

AT THE BUILDING in question, Harley quickly unloaded the dogs and sensed a certain amount of trepidation and fear in them. "It's okay, guys. You're with me this time," he murmured, reaching down a hand to gently stroke the two of them. Both appeared to lean against his thighs, gaining comfort from his touch.

"This time we're on the side of good. We'll go in and take a look at just what's going on here. And see if Jimmy's here. It would be easier here than at the compound under heavier security." But Harley didn't know exactly what the warehouse security had planned for him. He walked up to the front door and tested the door, but it was locked.

Figuring as much, he moved around to the back, looking for any entrance. The dogs growled, as he got around to the back door. He tested it, but it was locked too. He studied the dogs to find them staring at windows. He crept to the closest window and peered in; it seemed empty inside, but the window itself wasn't locked. He quickly jiggled it free and opened it up enough that he could hop inside. Both the dogs jumped in after him. And, with that, their noses went down to the ground, and the growling started. "Easy. We can't give away our position."

With a hand gently on each muzzle—to keep them calm—the trio quickly moved out to search the downstairs area. He found nothing overtly suspicious on the ground floor. It was empty, except for a lot of sealed crates and empty tables laid out in one room, but nothing to say exactly what it was that the men had been doing here. And, with that, Harley moved toward the stairs. As he approached, the hairs on the back of the female lifted. "Queen, what's the matter?" he murmured and crouched beside her. She growled a low warning, deep in the back of her throat.

"Got it. Trouble up ahead. Something's up there, and it's something you don't like."

He looked over at Bowser, and his teeth were bared, the whites of them shining in the darkness. "Neither do you. Interesting. We need to get up there and take a look."

He had one handgun with him. He quickly pulled it free of his holster, and, moving up the stairs, one at a time, with the dogs at his side, he got to the top landing, where a door was. It wasn't latched, and, on the other side, he heard a voice. But he couldn't hear anything distinctive. He listened quietly and then nudged the door open ever-so-slightly with his boot.

At that, the voices became louder but still indistinct.

"Here goes nothing." He pushed open the door a little wider and stepped inside. He saw no immediate sign of anyone. He was in what seemed like a butler's pantry area, with a big industrial-type kitchen off to the side. He moved through the pantry and into the kitchen, headed toward the voices. As soon as he came up to a corner, he peered around, and there he saw Jimmy, tied up in a chair. His eyes were frantic, and he kept shaking his head, but he had a cloth over his mouth, so he couldn't say anything. Beside him was another tied-up man, bloody, with obvious injuries to his face.

As Harley watched the other man receive another heavy blow, he studied the poor guy for a long moment—then realized it's the one he had taken Queen from. Harley sighed. Not what he wanted. That guy should have run farther than he did.

The attacker snorted. "Lie to me, will you?" And he smacked the handler hard against the side of his face. But the man was already unconscious. And his body just shifted to the side, without it being a noticeable blow.

Harley heard the dogs growl again, and he placed a hand on their heads to calm them down, as he peered ahead to see if anybody else was around. Pulling the dogs back, he quickly shifted them, coming around on the far side, finding nobody else was in here on the second floor of the big warehouse, as far as Harley could see.

As he came up to the front door to the kitchen, he thought he heard a sound ahead. He quickly pulled the dogs back, but Queenie was just ahead of him. Harley heard somebody call out to her.

"There you are. Jesus Christ. We've been looking for you everywhere. Come here," he called out to the dog.

Instead of wagging her tail, Queen growled.

"What's fuck is wrong with you?" the guy snapped. "Do you know how many people have been looking for you? At least you had the sense to come home."

Someone else, just out of Harley's vision, said, "You know that, if you yell at them, the dogs get quite pissy."

"I don't give a fuck if they get pissy or not. They can listen and behave themselves, or else we can just shoot the damn things."

"That'll put you in the same hot seat as Charlie over there."

"That's bad news. He'll kill him at this rate," he snapped.

"You want to tell him that he should stop?"

"Hell no. Better Charlie than me."

"Exactly. How long do you think he'll keep this up?"

"Too long. I don't think he even knows that he's hit that point yet."

"That's because he's just busy killing. When he gets like this, it's always ugly."

"I know." The man's voice drifted closer, as the one guy tried to get Queenie to go to him. Harley reached down a hand and quickly unbuckled the lead on her collar. She walked forward with her head down, but her tail was between her legs.

"Come on, girl. Come on. Let me get this back on you."

At that, the dog backed up.

"Get over here," the guy snarled at Queenie. "You wait until I get my hands on you, goddammit!"

Queenie backed up more, getting close to Harley again.

He stepped out, with Bowser at his side too. "Yeah, what will you do when you get your hands on her again?" he sneered. "Obviously she knows an asshole from a decent man."

The two men looked at him in shock. "Who the hell are you?" one of them asked.

"I'm the one who brought the dog back, but she doesn't want anything to do with you."

"Well, you just hang on to her here long enough for me to get this lead on her, and I'll teach her who's boss."

The guy stepped forward, not seeing Harley as a threat, only the dog. Harley held the dog gently for a long moment, as one of the two men approached. The other guy was watching, a sneer on his face. "The damn dogs are such a pain in the ass."

"Yeah, why is that?" Harley asked curiously. He was waiting for his chance to take down these assholes.

"They're always in trouble. They never do as they are supposed to, and, just when you think that they're on your side, they turn on you. That female bit me not very long ago. I've just been looking for a chance to get payback with her."

At that, the guy who had reached down for Queenie, turned back to look at his buddy, making the mistake of taking his eyes off her. "Right, she needs a good lesson."

Instinctively Queen jumped and bit hard, snapping down on the guy's wrist, while trying to snap a lead on her. Harley couldn't unhook Bowser because of the cone on his head. And Harley didn't want Bowser to reinjure himself. But Harley stepped forward to help Queenie take down the asshole. With his right, he gave a hard uppercut to the man's jaw. The guy seemed surprised, and, for a moment, his eyes rolled up in the back of his head. Then he went down.

"What the fuck?" the other guy snapped. "What the hell

are you doing?"

"Well, the dog *was* trying to bite him," Harley explained, eyeing the gun in this other guy's hand. "And you'll just shoot me because of the dog?"

"Yeah, damn right I'll shoot you," he snapped. "But, if we do anything to disturb the boss right now, there'll be hell to pay, so you just sit tight. Don't move."

"I'm not moving." He looked down at Queenie. "Attack."

Queenie immediately raced forward, and the gunman backed up, turning the gun on her. "You fucking bitch." But as he went to fire, Queenie jumped up, grabbed his gun hand at the wrist, and bit down hard. He shrieked in pain, but Harley was there with a second uppercut, and the gunman went down. Harley grabbed the man as he fell downward, so he would not make more sounds as he hit the ground.

With Queenie at his side, and Bowser still attached on a leash, Harley looked down on the cone and realized it could hinder the dog, and he couldn't defend himself. He quickly unhooked the plastic cone around his neck and took off the lead. And, with both dogs unleashed at his side, he crept forward because it now got deadly silent.

As Harley turned around the corner to where he'd seen Jimmy and the other man, the attacker stood between the two, holding two handguns, one in each hand, pointing them against both men's heads.

He looked at Harley, smiled. "Now which one of these guys do you give a shit about? Because he'll be the first to go."

CHAPTER 10

JASMINE PACED THE house forward, back, forward, and then back again. The deputies had been and gone, when she had nothing more to offer, and neither had they. She'd sent message after message after message to Harley and was getting nowhere. She'd even called the hospital, only to get confirmation that her mother had broken her hip. And she would be hospitalized. Jasmine strode outside once again to the front of the house to see absolutely nothing. She kept waiting for Harley to show up; she kept waiting for her son to show up. She kept waiting for Harley's white rental, the sheriff, somebody.

But, so far, it was just nothing.

She knew the sheriff and some local authorities were out looking for her son. She knew that some confrontation was going on somewhere, and she knew that a SWAT team was supposedly looking for the warehouse property that Harley had brought up. But none of it mattered; she just wanted her son back. And although she wanted her mother to be safe and looked after, her son was her priority, and that just made her feel even worse. How could she be so sure and yet so guilt-ridden and confused at the same time?

Finally she put on the teakettle and sat down on the front porch with a cup of tea and waited. "Surely he won't be too much longer."

When the phone rang, she answered it. "Hi, Chester," she said wearily. "Any news?"

"Harley's been seen inside the warehouse. We do have a team in place, but nobody's willing to take a shot, not until we know more."

"Harley is in there? What about my son?"

Chester took a deep breath. "He's there too."

"Oh my God." She bolted to her feet. "You've confirmed he's in there?"

"Yes, I can also confirm that he's been tied to a chair."

She gasped in shock. "I don't understand why. What's going on?"

"We don't have all the players ID'd yet, but do you remember Runal?"

"Yes, we went to school with him."

"Yeah, I think I can only say at this point that he's the one holding your son."

She stopped and gasped. "Are you serious?"

"Yes, why?"

"Nothing really, except"—her mind was frantic, as she thought back to that party—"Runal was giving me trouble. I was looking to leave the party because of him."

"Do you think he's the one who raped you?"

"I don't know."

"Because that brings up an entirely different question."

"What?" She wasn't linking the pieces together like he seemed to think she should.

"What are the chances that he's Jimmy's father?"

She sagged into a chair, closing her eyes and groaning. "Oh my God."

"And, in which case, then what if that's why Jimmy was kidnapped?"

"That's not fair. I shouldn't have to deal with this stuff right now."

"What if he knows he's his son?"

"Or thinks that he might be his son, you mean," she snapped back.

"You know Jimmy does have slightly darker skin."

"He's always outside in the sun," she said automatically.

"And he has black hair."

"You were fine to believe it was Harley's child, but now you're trying to make it look like maybe he was Runal's son."

"Well, Runal has a white mother and a Mexican father, so genetics can be difficult to spot. But, if you think that there's a good chance that he might have been the one who had dosed you with the date-rape drug, then there's also a good chance that he is Jimmy's father. If he knows he's Jimmy's father, that could be why he's kidnapped him."

"Or he's trying to get information to see if he's his child," she said quietly. She took a long slow deep breath. "If he is his child, then what?"

"I hate to say it, but there are father's rights."

She stared at her phone, shocked. "Surely that's not a thing," she cried out, "when I was raped."

"The thing about having this discussion now"—his voice turned heavy—"God, I shouldn't even be doing this over the phone. The problem is, we only have your word to say that you were raped. I don't have a file to say you came in at the time. I have no forensic evidence, no DNA, no blood tests to show that you were given a date-rape drug. You know that his lawyers would easily say that you were drunk, that it was consensual sex, and that you kept his child from him all these years. So now that he's got him, he wants time with him."

The horror of unimaginable horrors facing her, she completely blanked out and didn't know what to say; her jaw opened and then snapped again. And she made a tiny squeaking noise as her lungs expanded in a panic.

"I know. I know. I know that's not what happened, but all I can tell you is that this would make sense as to why he's kidnapped Jimmy."

"Why though?" she asked, when she finally could speak. "Why not just stop and talk to him?"

"Because he probably assumes that you've told Jimmy other stories."

"And then why shoot at the house?" she asked.

"I don't know. Maybe it was intended for you. Not your mother."

"Meaning that, if he killed me, he could step forward as my son's father?" she whispered in an agonizing tone. "Isn't this the worst nightmare any mother could have?"

"It is. And all I can tell you is that we're working on it."

"And you need to work faster. No way that asshole is keeping my son. And I don't care who he is." As soon as she realized what was going on, Chester told her to go to the hospital and that he'd call her.

"I want to just sit here and wait for you to bring Jimmy home," she cried out into the phone.

"That won't help," Chester said. "I don't know how long this will last. All I can tell you is that we're here, and Jimmy's fine at the moment."

"That's not helpful," she screeched bitterly into the phone.

"No, no, it isn't. And until we can get this resolved, I don't want you anywhere near this place. But now I do not want you sitting at home either, incapable of doing anything.

Go to the hospital. Look after your mother." And, with that, he hung up on her.

She'd sat here for the longest time and then too realized that sitting here really wouldn't help because she couldn't do anything. Yet it was almost like she was paralyzed. It was just beyond mind-boggling that something could even possibly be this ugly. But apparently there were father's rights that she hadn't even considered coming back around. Because of the rape, she'd assumed that she would be allowed full access and that the father would never be.

As she walked to her laptop and started researching her horror of horrors, she found, in many states, that was not the case. Facing something so incredibly horrible, she had absolutely no way to calm her mind, and she just sat here on the couch now, her knees against her chest, thinking about the implications of what had just happened. And all because Harley had walked back into her life, and it suddenly became public knowledge that he wasn't Jimmy's father. She shook her head. "I'm so damn glad you finally came back," she murmured, "but, good Lord, please don't leave me in this mess again."

It was not his fault in any way, and she knew that, but just the thought of the man who raped her trying to get her son on his side and that her boy had been even this close to that slimy bastard was enough to make her skin crawl. She took a long slow deep breath and then slowly thought about what she could do. She pulled out her phone, and it took a long time to distill what she knew into a text, but she just hoped that it was even possible that Harley saw it.

But she explained that Runal was potentially one of the men in the warehouse building with Jimmy and could be the man who raped her and, therefore, Jimmy's father. And, with that, she hit Send and closed her eyes. She didn't know if she'd done the right thing or not, but damn it. Doing the wrong thing right now could kill her son and Harley. And, just as she cared twelve years ago, she cared now.

And somewhere, somehow, in the deep recesses of her brain, she'd always—even after all this time—still been waiting for Harley to come back to her. What a fool she was. And then she thought about it and realized that, no, she wasn't a fool. She had just found love once and had never seen anything even close to that again. It had been worth waiting for back then, and it was worth waiting for right now. All she had to do was make sure that both of those males came home to her, safe and sound again.

And she needed to check on her mother.

Groaning once again at the split in her emotions and her focus, she decided the walk to the hospital would help her mood and would give her body something to focus on, instead of all this stressful information.

By the time Jasmine walked into the emergency area at the hospital, her insides were twisted into knots, but sitting at home wasn't an option. But she kept checking her phone constantly to look for any updates. She texted Chester when she arrived at the hospital to tell him that she was here. The only thing she got back was **Good. No update.**

She sighed, walked inside, pulling back the hair that had come loose from her walk, and smiled at the receptionist. "Hey. Where's my mother?"

"She's still in emergency." Jasmine knew this woman vaguely and thought her name was Sandy. "You can go down and see her though."

"Thanks." She walked toward the double doors into the curtained-off sections, caught sight of three doctors coming out from one closed curtain. "I'm Jasmine Willoughby, and I'm looking for my mother, Matilda," she said. "She came in with a broken hip."

The doctor immediately nodded and pointed to the bed he'd just left. "She's in there, but I need to talk to you."

She froze at that and then nodded. "How is she?"

"Not very good. She's definitely broken her hip, so that'll have to be fixed. She's also, at the moment, catatonic."

"Meaning, she's not responding?"

"Exactly." He frowned at her. "How long has she been like that?"

"She's been getting worse over time, and she remains at her home. She's under her doctor's care." And she named the doctor. "We're just trying to help her get along as much as we can."

"Well, she's not very good at the moment at all. It'll remain to be seen how she progresses moving forward."

Jasmine's face fell. "I'm not sure exactly what you're saying."

"I'm saying that I'm not sure she's capable of going home to be looked after. So far, she requires full care from a medical team here. She might need to go into a nursing home."

"I don't think she has the money for that," Jasmine said quietly. "I know they're very expensive."

"I understand, but sometimes we have no other option. There are state-run options too, depending on the financial situation."

She took a long slow deep breath. "Let's not deal with that as a primary issue right now," she said hastily. "Let's try to get her back on her feet."

"The surgery won't be for a couple days at least. And

we'll have to run a bunch more tests. To make sure that she'll survive the surgery. Her blood pressure is extremely high, and some of her blood counts are way down."

She frowned at him. "She is under the care of a doctor. I do whatever he tells me to do, as far as looking after her."

He nodded. "How often is she lucid?"

"This morning she was lucid for a couple hours," she replied, "and then it seemed to completely slide south. And she hasn't been lucid again all day."

"And then yesterday?"

"She wasn't there for half of yesterday," she admitted.

"And the day before?"

Starting to feel defensive, as if he were attacking her for not having looked after her mother enough, she added, "She was more alert the day before that. She was due to go to the doctor tomorrow."

"I'll follow up with the doctor and take a look at her file. At the moment we need to see if she comes back out of this." And, with that, he turned and walked away.

Jasmine walked into the curtained section, where her mother was on a bed, her eyes closed. Jasmine walked over, picked up her hand, and whispered, "Mom," but she got no answer. There was no response. The nurse walked in just then, looked at her, and smiled. "Hey, Jasmine. How are you doing?"

"Hey, Carly. How is my mom?"

She just shook her head. "It looks like the dementia is kind of rough right now."

"She does have lucid days though."

"And something like this can make it better or can also accelerate the downward slide," she answered quietly.

Jasmine rotated her neck to loosen the knots. "What am

I supposed to do?"

"We'll wait and see how she is over the next couple days," the nurse said quietly. "And, if you need help finding a place for her in a home …" At that, she let her voice break off.

"Why can't I look after her at home?"

Carly shook her head. "We're talking quite possibly that she would need to be in the hospital for a few days, and then she'll need home care. It also depends on how mobile she'll be, as to whether she can get to the bathroom on her own and whether she's even cognizant of what's going on around her."

At that, Jasmine nodded slowly. "Meaning that you expect she could remain in this state, even with her hip fixed."

"That's possible. We're certainly not counting on that being the case, but it's a possibility. We won't know until we see how she survives the surgery."

"And that won't be for a few days?"

"No, not for a few days yet and not until after a bunch of tests."

"She doesn't even know me right now."

"She doesn't know anybody right now," the nurse said gently. "She's gone inside, where she's happier."

"That's just tough to see." Jasmine sighed "Yes, I've certainly seen her like this a lot more recently. It's one of the things I've contacted the doctor about several times. But he said her condition is declining, and there's not a whole lot anybody can do."

"And maybe he's right. Maybe he's not. Again it's too early to tell. Let us run some tests and see how she is afterward." At that, the nurse turned and walked out.

Jasmine sat down on a chair beside her mother's bed, not

sure what she was even supposed to do here. Her world had been completely blown apart, what with her son in grave danger and now her mother's rapidly failing condition—not just in her physical health but also mentally.

Jasmine studied her mom intensely. It's like she'd given up. But then she was lying here, with a broken hip, and she had to be in extreme pain, and who would want to be cognizant of any of that? Or she'd been given painkillers and was now half in, half out of the present.

Jasmine sagged into the visitor's chair, wishing she had brought her laptop with her. She had her phone and started researching her mother's condition and special care homes. When somebody went into a private care home, the prices meant that her mother would probably go into a government-run one because the insurance wouldn't be enough. Was that such a bad thing? Jasmine didn't know.

She could almost hear her father's voice, telling her to look after her mother, which was fine and dandy, if that was even something she could do. But now she wasn't so sure. And her thoughts immediately went back to her son. Was he alive? Was he okay? Had they rescued him? And then she caught sight of her mother's slack features again. Jasmine realized just how caught she was, and had been, for a decade between the two of them. She murmured out loud, "You picked a nice time to leave, Dad." Of course he hadn't wanted to leave, so that just made her feel even worse. However, even if he were still here, would he have made the situation worse or better? She hesitated to answer that question. But, regardless, in his absence, everything had been dumped on her shoulders, when she felt least prepared for it all. She was just sixteen and newly pregnant. Even now, she was still a young woman and yet felt comparatively ancient.

Her mother was young too, in the sense that she could be looking at living twenty more years in a care home; Jasmine hoped not, for her mom's sake. Then again, if her mom was happy, then Jasmine shouldn't judge how her mom was getting on. But could anybody be happy in that state? She just kind of laid there; at least her eyes were closed, and it made it seem like she was sleeping, but Jasmine wasn't sure at all that her mother was.

Just then her mother opened her eyes and looked up at the hospital room. She rolled her head from side to side, as if checking out her space. When her gaze landed on her, Jasmine immediately bolted to her feet.

"Hey, how are you?"

Her mom looked up at her, as if she didn't understand the question, and just closed her eyes again.

Jasmine frowned, biting her bottom lip, as she sank back into her chair. This was devastating on so many fronts. She hoped for a change but was afraid that there wouldn't be any, when her phone rang. It was Chester. "Is he okay?" she asked instantly.

"He's still in the warehouse. I was just checking up on you."

"I'm fine," she said, with more fatigue in her voice than she expected. "I'm at the hospital, and my mom's condition is unchanged."

"I'm sorry. It's a tough spot to be in right now."

"Save my son, and everything else will become that much easier."

"We're working on it. Snipers are in position, but Harley appears to be an unknown factor in this equation."

"In what way?" she asked, but Chester hesitated. She murmured, "Hiding it from me won't help."

"Looks like they're in a standoff."

"Shit. Yeah, that sounds like Harley."

"Do you know any of his training since he's returned?"

"You mean, when he was gone?"

"Yes. We're arguing about his abilities to handle what's going on in there."

"He was a Navy SEAL," she replied quietly. "He's more equipped to handle what's going on in there than most of us. But that doesn't mean he's bulletproof."

"No, of course not. I'll get back to you." With that, he hung up.

She groaned, laid her head back, closed her eyes. "Harley, please don't screw up. This is the one time that I need you to be the best you can be and to save my son for me."

HARLEY STEPPED FORWARD with the dogs by his side.

The gunman smiled. "One more step and I pull both triggers."

"So you'll kill two men, and what did they ever do to you?" he asked quietly. He saw the terrified look on Jimmy's face as he glanced at him. But Harley deliberately didn't look at the kid's eyes. Harley looked down at the man already unconscious, probably beaten to death. "And that one's a waste of ammo."

"It's his fault, but now that I see both dogs are here, I might let him live."

"But these aren't your dogs," Harley said.

"The fuck they aren't," he snapped. "I paid good money for the one, and the other one was his way of getting into the game with me." He glared at Harley, daring him to disagree.

"The dog was supposed to be mine anyway. When he arranged it, he agreed that it was mine, and he would just handle it. But he didn't handle anything."

"That's because he didn't have any training to handle anything," Harley snapped back. "These aren't just dogs. These are military weapons. These animals need continuous training. They need to be worked properly. You can't just give them to anybody off the street and expect those guys to know what to do with them."

"Well, I did. And I gave him a chance to figure it out and to learn it. But what he did do was he ended up losing the damn dog to you. But now that you're back, I'll take the dog under my wing again."

"I don't think so." Harley tilted his head, eyeing the gunman. Harley could feel the frantic gaze of Jimmy on his face.

The killer stared at him. "I think I'm the one with the guns."

"You are, but that doesn't mean that you'll be the one who walks out of here. You might pull the trigger, but you won't leave alive."

Immediately the gunman switched his targets to the dogs. "I'll kill them first then."

"You can try." Harley tensed his muscles. "Again, you won't leave here alive."

"You'll kill me over a couple dogs?"

"I'll kill you over taking this boy."

At that, the guy looked at him in surprise, glanced at the boy, and started to laugh. "Here you thought he was your son, huh? Too bad I have to disappoint you in that regard."

At that, Jimmy's eyes widened, and he stared at Harley.

"I know he's not my son because I wouldn't leave his

mother in that condition. Of course you didn't have any such problem, did you?" Harley snapped back.

The gunman stared at him, frowning. "What the fuck do you know?" he asked.

"I know a lot, and so do the local authorities, and I understand that you were at the same party, where his mom was date-raped and ended up pregnant." He looked over at Jimmy. "Sorry you had to find out this way." He saw the shock in the boy's face. "I know it's not an easy way for a boy to find out that his mother was raped and that's how he came into existence. But true to form, she loves you, didn't treat you any differently, didn't make you pay for the sins of your father."

"Yeah, and I did wonder, when you came back into town, if this would end up happening. I figured that, before I got into trouble over it, I should at least get my son to come to know me."

"Interesting that you admit it." Harley's gaze narrowed, as he studied the gunman. He didn't appear to be heavily muscled or even looked to be in decent shape, but he'd seen guys who had fooled him before.

"Did you like the kitchen present?"

"Ah, so you're the one who shot through the window too. I wondered. The only thing that we could figure out that was different was the fact that I'd arrived in town, and the only reason anybody would care is if the rapist realized that the truth would come out."

"I don't give a shit about the rape. She was just one of many."

"Why? Because you couldn't get laid otherwise?"

At that, the gunman's gaze narrowed, and his face twisted with fury. "I can get all the women I want," he spit out.

"You just want an unresponsive woman, not anybody really participating, is that the idea?" Harley tried to keep his voice neutral, but inside he had a banked fury, itching to get out. He just wanted to get his hands wrapped around this guy's neck and to squeeze until he stopped moving.

"Maybe. It certainly saves on the bloody talk. All girls want is to be told that you *love* them," he said in disgust. "I love them for five minutes, while I'm banging them. After that, there's no way."

"That sounds about normal." Harley calmly judged the distance between them. "So what will you do now? You figure you'll kill them both? Or just the one and keep your son?"

"I haven't decided about my son yet. I was thinking that maybe it'd be good if we could spend some time together and see if he's like me at all."

"I can already tell you that he isn't."

"In which case, I might as well just pop him. Nobody'll ever prove he's mine anyway. Hell, I can't even know for sure."

"Except for DNA."

"If he's dead, nobody'll give a shit," he snapped. "And she can say all she wants about what happened back then, but she was as eager for me, as every other chick at that place."

"I don't think so."

"It's her word against mine. Nobody'll listen to a bitch. They're all the same. They just open their legs, want a good ride, and then afterward the bitches whine that you promised them something different," he sneered.

"They're all the same? Wow. You've really got a twisted view of females, don't you?"

"They are only good for one thing. I won't even have them in the kitchen. My chef is a hell of a lot better than any of those women."

"Yeah, interesting place you've got up there at the compound, digging a tunnel underneath to the Canadian border or something." Harley used his wild volley shot to distract the gunman, while Harley figured out what was going on. He saw a red light of a laser scope moving through the room. Definitely some attention outside was on them, but the question was, whose side was the sniper on? Harley didn't know yet.

"What the hell do you know about my place?" the guy straightened up, moving the guns to point at him directly. "I'll just shoot you. I'll fire into the dogs fast enough."

"You might get one off, but you won't get a second one." Obviously the gunman didn't like Harley's bravado.

The gunman kept staring at him. "I don't understand what you're after, man. Why the hell do you even give a shit?"

"Because, for one, what you did to Jasmine was a really shitty thing. She was my girl."

"But you left. The old man ran you out of town." He started to laugh at that. "And now look at you. Trying to come back as some hero. Once you run out with your tail between your legs, you're always the guy who ran away with his tail between his legs."

"Hardly that." Tilting his head to the side, he considered how he could release the dogs and take down this guy without any of the four of them getting shot. The odds weren't on his side. "That's not quite true, but you'll believe whatever the hell you want to anyway."

The other guy sneered. "I spent my life listening to assholes like you, hearing about them, how they were all guys in the military and were supposed to be so great. They're just losers. It's all about money. It's all about who's got power. It's all about strength. You gotta strong-arm the world into believing that you're the boss. Once you lose control of that, you lose control of everything. And that's what happened to you. You ran away, and now you come back, first thinking that he was your son, whining and bellyaching about it. Then you find out that he's my son, and you're upset because she spread her legs for me." He laughed. "The kid's mine, whether you like it or not."

"I get that, but I don't hold it against the kid." Harley quietly looked down at Jimmy, with a reassuring smile. But Jimmy was terrified, and it was obvious the conversation was getting to him as well. "You think that this will all just go away? That you'll shoot me, and you're good? Shoot the three of us, and you're good? Shoot the two dogs, and who gives a shit? You think you'll go back to your little compound, and nobody will give a damn?"

"I pay damn good money to make sure that nobody gives a damn. Why do you think nobody even knew about me functioning up in this corner of the world? I had to have a private place to get big enough to get anywhere, but I'm almost there. I'm making a deal to go across the country. Pretty soon it'll be me handling huge areas, not just my little corner of the world."

"That's too bad. I mean, that's a sign of your innocence, thinking that any of the big guys will play with you, because they won't. Nobody'll share with you. They'll just pop you one and take over your operation."

"No fucking way," he yelled in outrage. "I've been working for years to get their trust."

"Sure, but now they've got some problems with your trust, don't they? I mean, now there's talk about problems in your corner of the world, and now they're not sure that you're capable of handling this. And it doesn't take much to throw these guys off. You know for a fact that they don't like any confrontations locally. *Head down and don't cause attention* is the MO. But there'll be a hell of a confrontation coming up, and you're done for. You just haven't seen the writing on the wall yet."

"To hell with you," he snapped.

"No thanks," he said cheerfully. "But I want you for what you did to poor Jasmine."

He sneered again. "It was great. I loved banging that chick."

"No, you didn't bang her. She was unconscious. What you did was rape her. It's too bad she's not here right now so that she could kick your ass into the ground for what you did, but it's also a good thing she was unconscious the whole time. So that she doesn't have the nightmares that you would love for her to have."

"I gave her the best time of her life." He laughed. "No matter what you think." He sneered and added, "That chick didn't know how good she got it."

"There's no point in talking to an idiot like you." He took a step forward, meaning for the guns to confront him again. That way they weren't pointed at Jimmy.

"Don't move. No fucking way. I'm not so stupid that I'll let you pull a trick like that."

"No? What will you do about it?"

"Oh, don't you even think that I won't. I've got all kinds of things I'll do to you, but it'll start with a bullet between your eyes."

Just seeing that trigger finger clench and the muscles of the forearm tighten, Harley dove forward to the ground as fast as he could and rolled between the two men's chairs, so Harley came up right at the gunman's feet. Instead of standing up, Harley jerked the gunman's left leg out from under him, his shots going wild, as the gunman tried to shoot Harley, not expecting him to jump to the floor. And he fired again and again, but, at this point, his gun was leveled at the ceiling, and the dogs were on him.

Between the sound of the dogs growling and barking and trying to help as Harley was giving orders, it was chaos. Finally he managed to pin the gunman to the floor. Harley heard shots fired and voices outside and had no idea what was going on, but he didn't dare take his focus off this asshole. He managed to wrestle the guns away from him, until the two spun harmlessly from them.

And, even with the dogs getting in the way, the gunman managed to clock Harley slightly on the jaw. He shook his head, turned back to the gunman, received another clip to his jaw, but this time Harley flipped him over and sat on his back, his hands in his vise grip. Harley ordered both dogs to Stop and Guard. Both of them sat, their butts down and stared at Harley, but then they turned their gazes quickly to the asshole on the ground.

Harley took a long slow deep breath. "Okay, now everybody calm down." He looked over to see the one guy was still unconscious and back to see Jimmy staring at him. He pulled his pocketknife from his back pocket, but he first had to secure the guy on the ground.

"Hang on a minute there, Jimmy. I've got to make sure that this guy is safely secured. We don't want him loose anymore."

As he shifted his weight, the guy underneath him bucked up hard and twisted. Then his fist came up, slamming into Harley's jaw, hard enough to piss him off. And the fight was on again. It took several more minutes and the dogs jumping on the guy's shoulder to secure him again. Harley rolled him over, and this time he snapped, "You don't even get a chance this time!" He belted him hard with an uppercut to the jaw. The guy groaned and sagged to the floor. Not sure it was enough, Harley gave him a second blow, then quickly flipped him over, pinned his hands behind his back, and looked around for something to tie him up with. The only thing he had was what was currently tying the other two men.

He stood, ordered the dogs to Guard, raced over to Jimmy, quickly cut the ties on his hands, and used that rope to secure the gunman on the floor. With that done, he walked over to Jimmy, bent down in front of him, removed his gag, cutting his feet free now. "You okay?"

Jimmy looked at him, fear in his eyes, his bottom lip trying hard to hold tight.

Harley grabbed the kid and pulled him into his arms, giving him a big hug. "It's okay. We've got you now."

Jimmy sniffled slightly, gave him a big squeeze, and then stepped back. "Is what he said true?"

"Which part?" Harley asked, as he walked over to the injured handler and quickly cut his ties.

"About him being my father."

"There's a damn good chance, yes," He looked over at Jimmy, who looked like he wanted to cry. "Remember. You're not responsible for your father's actions," he murmured. "Your mother certainly never held it against you. She loves you."

"How could she even stand to look at me?" he asked, tearing up.

"Because, even though the way you came to be isn't what anybody would ideally wish for, your mother loved you right from the beginning, when you were still growing in her belly. She refused to have an abortion, despite your grandma and your grandpa pressuring her to do that. She was only sixteen, but she held firm with her parents. She chose you over them. Jasmine would never have done anything to hurt you. She didn't even tell me about what happened, until I got back here. She didn't tell anyone after that first few weeks, when she tried to make people listen to her, and nobody would."

"And that was likely because of Granddad, wasn't it?"

"It was partly your granddad, yes," he agreed, with a nod. "The thing is, you can't blame people who have gone before us because we can't understand where they came from nor how they learned the lessons that they did nor the shoes that they walked in themselves. So it's easy to blame everybody else. This is where we stand on the side of right, and we'll do the best we can to go on from here." Harley smiled at the kid, standing strong. "Jimmy, you've done really well so far. So take a deep breath, calm down, and realize that we'll get through this. After all, we survived, and your mom will be really excited about that."

And just then another man entered the room and called out, "I don't think so." And another gunman appeared. He looked at Harley and at the guy trussed up on the floor. "Put your hands up over your head."

Harley slowly raised his hands. "Who the hell are you?" But he knew. That's what the gunfire outside was about. The cops had seen this guy trying to enter the warehouse and had tried to stop him. But didn't obviously.

"I'm the guy who shot through the kitchen window. I was hoping to take out the stupid bitch who gave birth to this kid. Instead I guess I mistook her for the old lady and missed anyway."

"Well, she's a little hard to pin down these days. Her mental state's not very good." Harley looked over at Jimmy, at the gunman on the floor, and the injured man. "So I suppose you're here for this guy, are you?" And he nodded at the gunman down on the ground.

"Maybe not." He contemplated his options.

At that, Harley just waited. Another element had entered, and Harley couldn't exactly be sure what was going on.

Then the second gunman lifted his arm and fired once.

CHAPTER 11

JASMINE SAT AT the hospital, her body frozen in time. Too bad her mind wasn't frozen, as it raced from one horrific outcome to another in an endless loop of nightmarish proportions. Her mother had not moved; her phone had not rung, nor had she gotten any answers from the medical teams. The nurses had come and gone; the doctor had come and gone. Jasmine still knew nothing more. When her phone rang, the Caller ID read Chester. "What's up?"

"Well, things have changed hands," he said quietly. "We haven't gone in. Your buddy took care of the original gunman. Your son is safe, but now we've got another shooter involved, who gained access via the roof of the warehouse and dropped down inside. He then pulled out a handgun and has pinned Harley and your son inside the place. We just heard a shot a few minutes ago."

"Jesus," she cried out. "Who got hurt?"

"We don't know, but it's not your son, and it's not Harley. They are still standing."

She sagged in relief into her chair. "Seriously?"

"Yeah. So, although we're one step further, we're still not out of the woods yet."

"Do you know how hard this is?" she murmured.

"I was of two minds whether I should call and tell you. Believe me. I'm going against protocol by even letting you know."

"Well, I appreciate it, but I still need both of them home safe."

"We're working on that," Chester said drily. "So far Harley's got both dogs, and they appear to be taking care of business on their own, which is why we've held off shooting. The minute we start firing bullets in there, it can get ugly. And we can't necessarily control who dies because we don't have a clear line of sight for the shots. And we have to have that before we can take out anybody."

"No! I don't want bullets going wild in there," she said, her heart in her throat. "We need to save both of them—and those dogs."

"I'll let you know as I learn anything more."

When he hung up, she sagged back into her seat. She wanted to go down there, but, at the same time, getting in the way wouldn't help.

The doctor stepped in at the moment, smiled at her. "She'll stay here overnight. Why don't you go home, get a shower, get some rest, some food? You can always come back later, but she'll be sedated for the pain. We have the x-rays back. We've got the blood tests, and we're doing a couple more tests, just to make sure that she's cleared for surgery. But, other than that, not a whole lot you can do right now."

She smiled and thanked him. "I appreciate that. Maybe I will go home."

"Do. You need a break."

"I know." She yawned. "Just so much craziness is going on."

"Right. You're involved in that shootout that's currently happening, aren't you?"

"Yes," she said quietly, "and not in a nice way."

"Let's hope they resolve it safely."

"I just want my son and my boyfriend back again." She stopped at her own words, shook her head, then muttered, "I need to leave." She stumbled out to the front of the hospital and stood here, wondering what had possessed her to say that because, damn it, none of this made any sense.

Outside, she took a long slow deep breath, realizing that, for the first time in a long time, she wasn't looking after her mother. She didn't quite know what she was supposed to do with herself. She slowly turned and walked toward home. She wanted to head back in the direction of where the shooting was, and, even as she realized that she had no business going there, her feet turned in that direction anyway. By the time she arrived, a huge perimeter blocked off the chaos happening nearby. She stepped forward, wondering where Chester was.

Then he caught sight of her. "What the hell are you doing here?" he roared, coming toward her.

She stared at him blankly. "I didn't know where else to go. My whole life's here."

He groaned, reached out, gave her a quick hug. "Look. I need you to just stand back."

"Why?"

"Because of the newest gunman inside, and we've repositioned our snipers. We'll try and take him out."

She looked up at him in horror. "But you'll miss. You don't know what Harley'll do. You don't know what two War Dogs will do. You don't know how any of this will work out," she wailed. "Please don't do that."

"We have to," he replied quietly but firmly. "He shot at one of our guys before he slipped inside. This can't keep on."

And, with that, he parked her firmly outside the perimeter. "Stay here."

Then he turned and raced back to his colleagues. She stood in shock and pain, as she watched while everybody set out for this operation that she had no clue how to stop. She just knew that, if it went forward, it would be bad news for everyone. With her heart in her throat, she could do nothing but stand here and wait.

HARLEY'S HANDS WERE still up, and Jimmy was now tucked up close to his side, with the two dogs sitting here, one on either side of himself and Jimmy—both of them growling. Harley stared at the gunman, wondering what the hell the new game was.

"Perfect. Now that asshole won't be on my case anymore."

Harley shifted his gaze to the gunman he had tied up on the ground. But no sense worrying about him at this point, as he was dead. The bullet had gone in through his head and had blown part of it off. Since this dead guy was potentially Jasmine's rapist, Harley felt justice had been served. And now the new gunman stared at Harley, with a smile on his face. "Really?" Harley asked. "You just wanted to kill him?"

"Not just him. I'm number two in the organization, and this is perfect timing for me to take over. Been planning it for a while. This asshole doesn't even realize someone was taking over his hand. There was already some concerns about his ability to control himself. All he would do is rape the women around him, but he couldn't even do that quietly, where the women wouldn't scream, so he had to drug them all. That's when he started to lose his business. And his women. Sometimes they didn't survive." The stranger shook his head. "Runal's such a slime ball. I had a little conversation with his distribution network, and we decided he was a liability to us all. This is perfect timing to take him out."

"And us?" Harley asked quietly.

He hesitated. "Sorry, you're really in the wrong place at the wrong time."

"I get that, but do you really have to shoot the kid too?"

He looked over at Jimmy. "He's Runal's kid, isn't he? So seriously he shouldn't be allowed to live. He might want to come back into the organization another day. We can't have that."

"He's eleven," Harley said in disgust. "You're worried about a kid coming after you in eight years?"

"No, not really. But you know that the bosses won't like it if I leave anybody behind."

"Maybe." Harley waited for the stranger to divert his gaze, then Harley used hand signals to alert the dogs to an upcoming command.

The stranger was focused on the dogs and nodded. "I should get those two back though," He looked at the window. "I wonder if I can get them to jump out."

"Probably from the first floor. You don't want to injure them or kill them. Then they are useless to you. Plus, you need to give them the right order. And you've got to make sure you don't shoot them," Harley said sardonically. "They're very susceptible to bullets."

"Yeah, but one of them, the female there, she's had some decent training. The other one's a new element, but dogs are really important to the security of our place." The gunman stared at the window beside him; it was about waist high. "So the windows on the ground floor are the same?" he asked, waving his gun in Harley's direction.

"Yes."

"And you know the proper orders to make these dogs work?" he asked, eyeing Harley.

"Yes."

"Then move out to the first floor." With his gun hand waving them toward the stairs, Harley pushed Jimmy ahead of him, had him down the stairs first. Harley followed, with the dogs following him. The gunman took up the rear.

"Any of you get any ideas about bolting, I'll shoot the kid."

All of them arrived safely on the ground floor.

Then the gunman chose a window, glad to see it was also waist high. "I'll need you"—he waved that gun again toward Harley—"as my shield to get outta here and to work the dogs." He turned toward Jimmy. "Sorry, kid." Then he leaned over and called, "Come on. Come here, girl." He patted the windowsill, as if to show her what he wanted.

Queenie whined and then her whine turned to a growl and back to a whine.

"Hang on," Harley said. "Let me see if I can get her over the window."

He walked a little closer, and the gunman immediately turned the gun on him. "No tricks."

"Nope. I just don't want you to shoot the dogs. They've had enough abuse."

"No, I won't shoot anybody who's been abused," he said, with a sneer. "That's just stupid."

"True." Harley called the dogs closer.

As they came with him, the gunman nodded. "Perfect. Get them to jump out the window."

"And, of course, you won't shoot me if I do it, right?" he

asked in a dry tone.

"I'm afraid your life is already on the line. You'll either get shot by me or by the cops outside. There's absolutely nothing I can do about that. If I could, I'd let you take the kid and run, but you know that ain't possible."

And, of course, given his criminal lifestyle and the people he worked with, it wasn't possible. But, at the same time, Harley had no intention of letting Jimmy take a bullet that he didn't deserve. "The kid doesn't know anything, and he's innocent. He just watched a man pretty well get beaten to death in front of him. Then you shot your boss in his view too. He'll need a shrink after this, as it is."

"Is Charlie dead up there?"

"I'm not sure, but he certainly hasn't moved in the last couple hours."

"Shit, he was decent too, but I don't have time to look after him. So get the dogs up here."

Using verbal commands, Harley ordered the dogs up onto the window and outside. As soon as they went outside, the gun came up. "Now you turn around and go back to the kid."

As Harley turned, Jimmy was right there beside him. In fact, he was standing behind him.

"Don't hide behind him. Step away, kid."

Harley looked down at Jimmy, then at the gunman. "You could still let the kid go."

"He's too old. If he was younger, maybe. But, at this age, I can't. He'll just tell."

As he went to raise the gun, Harley yelled, "Attack!" Then he covered Jimmy with his body.

Both dogs jumped through the window and lunged at the gunman. He shrieked, his gun going off, as he turned to twist away from them, but his arm was still too high and missed both dogs and fired aimlessly into the air. Harley pushed Jimmy to the floor and was already pounding the gunman into the ground, while the dogs each had bitten down on the gunman's shoulders.

When Harley finally got the dogs to calm down, the new guy was unconscious beside him. He grabbed his phone, tossed it to Jimmy. "Call the sheriff outside. They're lining up for a sniper shot."

Jimmy stared at Harley in shock. "They are?"

"Get down. Get down," Harley said to Jimmy, as he had the dogs jump out the window again. Jimmy ducked but was still stunned and struggling to get the phone to work. "It's okay, Jimmy. We just don't want anything to happen at this point because the cops are finally doing something to get this guy out of here." Harley dragged the newcomer over and then out the window and took Jimmy with him as they followed suit.

"What if I started screaming?" Jimmy asked.

"Well, it might help. Might also get you a bullet."

At that, Jimmy shut up.

Harley grabbed his phone from Jimmy's fumbling fingers and called Chester. When the deputy answered, Harley explained, "It's clear in the warehouse. We're outside. We've got one severely injured inside, plus one dead inside. We got one injured outside. Both Jimmy and I are fine."

The deputy immediately shouted, "What?"

"Tell your men to stand down."

In the background, Harley heard Chester frantically yelling to call it off. Finally he came back on the line. "We're coming in."

"You can come in, but we're outside."

"Where are you?"

And they kept talking on the phone as Harley directed Chester to the side of the warehouse where they were.

As soon as Harley saw Chester, Harley shut off his phone, and Jimmy raced toward Chester.

Harley looked over at the deputy. "Hell of a nice small town you got here. Don't mind if I don't stay though."

"Given the ruckus you've kicked up since you got here," he snapped, "I'll cheerfully drive you to the border."

Right behind Chester, Harley saw Jasmine racing toward him, but she caught sight of Jimmy first and immediately threw her arms around her son and hung on tight.

Harley looked down at the two dogs, called them back, made them sit, and then lie down to relax. He sat right between them to make sure that nobody mistook them as threatening. As the deputy walked over and checked on the stranger, he handcuffed him, then looked at the dogs. "Are they dangerous?"

"Only if you're an asshole trying to do something wrong," Harley said tiredly.

"You know that, if you can control them, there's an awful lot of work for dogs like that."

"They're very valuable. I'm just not sure where and what I would need to set up shop with them."

"As far as assets go, you've got two of the best right there."

"I know." He reached a hand down to pet both dogs. They looked at him and leaned in. "Somewhere in the warehouse is a big white cone collar for Bowser, from the vet," he said. "Had to take it off him, so he had a chance to fight for his freedom."

"We'll get it." And the deputy dragged the latest gunman to his feet and led him away.

At that, an awkward silence grew around Harley. He rubbed his face. He looked up to see Jasmine, standing with her arms wrapped around her son, Jimmy. She mouthed *Thank you* to him.

He smiled, nodded. "You're welcome."

Jimmy turned around to look at him, his bottom lip still trembling. Harley got to his feet and opened his arms. The kid raced forward, and he closed them around him tightly. He just held him, while watching Jasmine, looking lost.

He opened an arm, and she came flying.

With both of them tucked up close, he just held them. His heart had never been quite so full, as he realized just how much he'd stood to lose.

"Don't ever do that to me again," she whispered.

He kissed her gently on the temple. "Wasn't planning on it this time either," he murmured.

Jimmy looked up at them. "I hope that never *ever* happens again." He looked toward his mother. "Is it true?"

Confused, she looked at him and then up at Harley. "Is what true?"

"The conversation about his heritage came up."

She winced. "All I can tell you is that I went to a party after Harley left. I was upset. I drank too much, and I woke up the next morning in not very good shape. It's obvious that something had happened, but I didn't know what. I found out months later that I was pregnant with you, yes. But I never blamed you for it. I never held it against you, and I don't care who your father is," she said in a firm voice.

Jimmy looked at her, tears in his eyes. "But, Mom, that's terrible."

"Of course it's terrible, but it also happened twelve years

ago, and I've come to deal with it."

He shook his head, looked up at Harley. "Why did you have to leave?"

"Because your mom was only sixteen," he said quietly. "She was still in school. I didn't have her parents' permission to marry her, and they told me to get the hell out. I needed to grow up myself, and then I was planning on coming back. Unfortunately it was a little too late. It seemed like time just got away from us, and then I didn't know how to get back."

Jimmy shook his head. "Now that you're back, are you staying?"

"That's a really good question. I'm not sure I want to stay in this town," he murmured, "but I know that your mother has ties here that she can't easily break."

Jimmy looked at his mom. "Like what?"

"Your grandmother for one," she said quietly. "What you don't know is that she fell, broke her hip, and she's in the hospital."

At that, Jimmy's gaze widened, and the unshed tears once again filled them. "That's not good. She's really harmless."

"She is," Jasmine murmured, looking up at Harley.

"It was a tough situation for everybody back then," Harley explained to Jimmy. "But what we do from now on is an entirely different story. It's up to us to make the future as we want it."

Jimmy looked at him and back to his mom. "I want you two to get back together again. I've had enough of not having a dad. And obviously I don't want the one who I was supposed to have," he declared, looking back at the warehouse. He shook his head. "I'll have nightmares for a long time."

"Yes." Harley nodded. "You might get nightmares, but you also saw what happened. You also know that some closure is there. Some justice is there too, and it helps that your mother has already put it behind her. So we won't upset her anymore by bringing it up when we don't have to. Right?"

"I can understand that. That doesn't mean I'm okay with what happened."

"I don't expect you to be," Harley said quietly. "But use that knowledge and that experience now to learn and to grow and to become a better person yourself."

Jimmy gave him a very adult look and nodded. "I can do that."

CHAPTER 12

JASMINE LOOKED UP at Harley, kissed him gently on the cheek. "I'm glad you finally came back."

He hugged her close, obviously choked up by her words. She just held the two of them, crushing her face against his chest. "Can we go home now?" she whispered. "It's been a really rough day."

Her son laughed, but there was a broken hiccup sound to it. "Man, I don't want to ever see a day like this again."

They stepped back slightly, so that Harley could move. She looked down at the dogs and then crouched against the first one, cuddled him gently, and whispered, "Bowser, you have my undying gratitude," gently scratching him at the top of his head, careful of his injuries around his neck. "We need to get that collar back on him again." Then she walked over to Queenie, who immediately wagged her tail and gave her a big welcome. "You too, sweetheart. I thank you so much for bringing my two best boys back to me, safe and sound."

Jasmine looked up at Harley. "Come on. Let's get the dogs home." As she turned to walk around the building, she watched a deputy come toward her, holding out the cone. She took it from him, with thanks. "I guess we have to give statements or something, don't we?" she asked Harley.

"Oh, yeah." Harley sighed and gave a pained groan. "There'll be tons of that to do."

She looked up at him and smiled. Then she reached across, handed him that cone. "Put this on Bowser, and let's go home."

"I'm hungry," Jimmy said out of the blue.

She stopped, looked at him. "Seriously?"

He gave her a bashful look. "Yeah. I am. How about pizza?"

She rolled her eyes because that was something that they only did on special occasions, when there was a bit of spare money. "Maybe."

"I think pizza is a great idea. Is that pizza place on Main Street still open?"

"Sure is," Jimmy said. "They have the best pizza."

"And I would agree with that. They have the best pepperoni," he murmured.

"And then they have extra-superlarge pieces," Jimmy continued," if you buy the family size." He looked over at his mom. "Mom, can we?" he pleaded.

She looked over at the two men in her life and smiled and laughed. "What about the dogs?"

"We can share with them," Jimmy said immediately.

She snorted. "That's not quite what I meant." She looked over at Harley. "Do you have enough dog food?"

"I certainly do for a while. Not an issue."

"Maybe, if we ordered it now, we could pick it up on the way home." She yawned. "I'll honestly go home and just crash for the rest of the night."

"That's the adrenaline crash," Harley explained.

"You and me both," Jimmy said, "but I want food first."

Harley shrugged. "It is a very good sign that the kid is hungry."

Jasmine groaned with a big grin on her face, as they

walked back toward the street. She looked up and down for Harley's vehicle. "Are we walking?"

"No. I've got the truck." He led the way to where he'd parked, and, while putting the dogs in the back seat, the rest of them loaded up in the front, and he joined them there and drove straight to the pizza joint.

"We didn't phone it in." She stared at Harley. "I don't think I'm up for waiting."

He smiled at her. "Just give me a minute." And he disappeared. She looked over at Jimmy and grabbed his hand. "I'm so glad that you're safe. You had me so worried."

"Me too. It was not fun to hear about what happened to you. I think that's terrible."

"It was certainly not much fun at the time." She gave him a sad smile. "But it's not your problem, and I dealt with it a long time ago."

"It still shouldn't have happened. It's not fair that people can do something like that and get away with it."

"According to you guys, he's dead now." She nodded. "And, I hate to say it, but maybe that's for the best."

He nodded. "I guess that it is. And I'm really glad that he's dead, but I kind of wanted to see him suffer first," he said in a hard voice.

"I get that too. I've thought about it many times over the years, but I've come to terms with it now, and it is what it is." She squeezed his hand. "Sometimes you don't get the closure you want, so you make do with the closure you have."

He smiled. "You're a better person than I am."

She laughed. "No, not at all. You are the best."

He shook his head and grinned at her. "And what about Harley? Are you keeping him?"

She burst out laughing. "Harley isn't exactly the kind of person you *keep*, like a dog or a pet."

"Maybe not, but I think he'd stay, if you could convince him to stay."

She shrugged, embarrassed. "I don't know about that," she said. "We have a history, but it was a long time ago."

"So maybe it's better that you forget that part and just start fresh because it's obvious he cares."

"And so do I," she admitted. "I just don't know if it's enough."

"It's enough. You haven't had much love in your life. You deserve so much more."

She looked at him in surprise. The comments that he sometimes made just seemed to come out of nowhere. "I've had a very good life," she said firmly. "You're all I ever needed."

"But, Mom, I'm growing up. In another seven years, I'll be eighteen."

She stared at him wordless because, of course, he was right. She knew that, but to even hear him talk in such an adult way was a sign of the times changing. "I don't know that I'll ever come to terms with that." She smiled.

"You will because you won't have a choice. I think you should marry Harley and have more kids."

She burst out laughing at that. "Well, don't mind if we don't let you rearrange our lives just quite so easily on us."

"You really should take my advice"—he grinned—"besides I really like him."

"He's a good man."

"He saved my life, you know? Several times he kept trying to talk both gunmen into not shooting me. Of course neither of the gunmen would listen, but it was really interesting to know that this stranger—who doesn't even know me—was prepared to go to bat and to take a bullet in my stead because of you."

She stared at him in amazement, while he told her what had gone on inside, although she was shocked at what her son had to go through. She knew that would be something he had to make peace with over time, and it wouldn't be easy, and she might have to even look at some counseling for him.

But she was in awe at what Harley had done. "I don't know that he did it so much for me, but he did it because you were important to me, yes, and you're also an innocent young man." She caught herself from saying *child* at the last minute.

"Maybe, but I know. I could just tell how much he cares about you."

"That's true," she said, "just like I care about him."

"So what's the problem?" Jimmy asked curiously, looking at her.

She smiled. "It's just not that easy."

"Absolutely it is. You guys need to just sit down and figure this out. Sounds like you've been apart for way too long." At that, he shuffled in his seat, leaned back, closed his eyes. "Let me know when it's time to eat."

"You'll just fall asleep?" she asked in surprise. "After all that you went through?"

"At least I'll rest a bit. And then I want to go home, eat as much as I can, and go to sleep. It's been a tough day, Mom."

"It has been." She watched, as he closed his eyes, her heart so big that it felt like her throat would close up. But she didn't even have a chance.

As she turned, the driver's side opened, and there was Harley, with two massive pizza boxes. She shook her head. "Who'll eat all that?" she gasped.

He looked at her in surprise. "Well, I'm pretty sure I will, and I'm pretty sure Jimmy'll give me a run for my money. Right, Jimmy?"

Jimmy stared at the boxes with avid greed. "I am. Let me take those from you." He reached across, snagged them out of his hand, and hugged them close. "Now, if we're not home in five minutes, I'll get started on these in the truck."

"No, you're not." Jasmine laughed. That set the tone as they headed home.

Once in the house, they headed right for the kitchen. The boxes were opened, napkins were brought out, and everybody dug in.

The dogs both peacefully sat to the side, watching intently. Jasmine looked down at the dogs, then over at Harley. "What will you do with them now?"

"I'm not sure. Your deputy friend suggested that there was an awful lot of need for well-trained dogs in law enforcement."

"Yes, I would think there is."

"So I might go into something like that."

Jimmy stopped eating, staring at them both. "Cool. That'd be sweet."

"It would, wouldn't it?" Harley nodded.

"You'll do it here?" Jimmy asked.

"Have to look into that. Depends on your mom."

"Why?" Jimmy asked in confusion.

"It depends whether she wants to stay here or not, whether she wants to move somewhere else."

At that, her throat closed up, and she stared at him. "Seriously?"

"I think I waited long enough to come back. So, unless you're telling me to leave again, I'll stay pretty damn close to your side, unless you've got any objections."

She stared at him in shock, and she heard Jimmy's *whoop* of delight beside her. She felt the tears heating up in the corner of her eyes. It had been a hell of an emotional day already.

She whispered, "No, I'm not telling you any such thing. I'm just not exactly sure where and what we're up to yet. I've only just gotten used to having you around."

"I wasn't planning on leaving, but I'm not exactly gainfully employed."

She snorted. "Neither am I. I think we're two peas in a pod."

He grinned. "I'm sure I can do better than what I've done these last few years, but I don't want to give up the dogs, so that also depends on you."

"Of course not." She looked at him in surprise. "They saved you guys' lives. I won't let them have anything but an absolutely wonderful life." She looked down and gently caressed Bowser's head inside the cone.

"There's also the problem of your mother."

"Yep, there is that, and I don't know what the answer is. The doctor did mention that she might need full-time care after this, but it's a wait-and-see scenario."

"That's sad." Jimmy reached for another piece of pizza and halfway through, he looked at it. "I'm actually getting full."

"Part of that's the adrenaline reaction." Harley studied him carefully. "The best thing you can do is go crash."

"I was thinking of that." Jimmy yawned, as he continued

to bite down on the pizza. When he finally finished, he stood, slowly bent down, gave his mom a quick hug. "I have to go. I'll be horizontal in two minutes."

She heard him stumble upstairs, and she looked over at Harley. "Are you sure he's okay?"

He nodded. "After stuff like this, people can react differently." He cocked his ear, as he listened to the footsteps overhead.

"I just don't even know if I'll ever sleep again," she whispered, feeling some of her own stress-related reaction settling in.

He grabbed her hand. "You don't have to be alone anymore. You know that, right?"

She gave him a misty smile. "I missed you so much. I hated you sometimes, but I always missed you."

"I get it. I should have come back earlier."

"Maybe it needed to happen this way. I don't know what I would have been like if you had come back five years ago. When I just even think about it, it's hard."

"I don't want to look back, if we don't have to. How about we just look forward?" He looked at the pizza, snagged a small slice. "And I think I have room for just one more."

"I can't believe you've eaten as much as you have."

The pizza in one of the boxes was completely gone, and the other was half gone. She'd had just three pieces, which was one past her normal. She smiled. "Are you crashing now too?"

"I need to shower. And we'll deal with the authorities and all the questions tomorrow, but it's late now. Are you okay to crash soon?"

She nodded. "I do have a spare room. Or there's my room."

He gave her a look; she flushed. "You don't have to," he said quietly.

She frowned at him. "I wouldn't if I didn't want to, and, no, this has absolutely nothing to do with what happened to me at the party. It has everything to do with what I wanted with you in the first place," she said crossly.

"You were the sweetest thing, and turning you down was the hardest damn thing I ever did in my life."

"I spent all that time wishing you hadn't," she said, "because my first time wasn't something I even remember—and I guess I'm grateful for that."

He winced. "Well, we can always make it better for you tonight."

"And here I thought you were tired," she said, with a teasing grin.

"I'll never be too tired for that." He stood. "Will this bother you?" He held out his left hand.

She looked at him in surprise. "Of course not. How could it possibly?"

"Well, I'm not a whole man." He quietly studied her intently.

"You are more whole, even in this shape, than any other man I know," she murmured gently. "So don't ever let that be part of our discussion."

"Has Jimmy ever mentioned it?"

"Honestly, I'm not sure he's even noticed."

He smiled, nodded. "That's a compliment then."

"Oh, yeah, it is. I might miss that arm if it wasn't attached, and I couldn't get a hug. but the other one still works."

He burst out laughing, stood up, tugged her to her feet, wrapped her up in both arms, and squeezed her gently. She could feel the difference in the pressure from one to the other. "It's a pretty advanced prosthetic."

"My boss's wife designs these. She's come a hell of a long way. She's starting to get national recognition for her work. We're all very grateful to her. There's still a way to go, but she's determined to give us the best she can."

"And she's doing that for Badger?"

"She's also missing a leg," he admitted.

"Wow." She stared at him.

He grinned. "You'd love them both. I can't wait for you to meet them."

"Will I get a chance to meet them?"

"Oh, I think so." He grabbed her hand and led her to the stairs.

"Don't you have to take the dogs out for the night first?"

He stopped, thought about it. "That's a good idea." He released her hand, took them out in the backyard, gave them big bowls of food and water, and, by the time the dogs were taken care of, and he headed back upstairs, catching her as she stepped from the shower, a towel wrapped around her head. He asked, "Mind if I have a shower too?"

"Go right ahead."

He smiled. "Then I'll be ready in a few minutes. I've just got a lot of sweat and grime to take off."

She walked into her room and sat on the edge of the bed. Not only had she not had sex that she remembered but she hadn't been with any man since her rape. The only man she'd ever wanted to be with was the one who was in the shower right now. She was nervous, excited, torn, and, at the same time, couldn't wait. She'd wanted him since forever, when her hormones had first kicked in, and he'd done nothing but refuse her at every turn.

She now realized what it must have cost him to have been so honorable back then, but she would do everything she could to shake that into the trash can where it belonged now.

When he returned and walked toward her, with just a towel wrapped around his waist, she wondered at the look in his eye and then realized that he didn't have on his prosthetic. He had part of a stump on his upper arm, but that was it. The shoulder itself was damaged and missing a lot of muscle. She hopped to her feet, tears in her eyes, as she walked over. He immediately backed up; she shook her head, leaned forward, and kissed him where the stump was.

"My God," she said, "the pain you must have been in."

He caught her up in his right arm, crushed her close to him, and whispered, "Did I ever tell you how much I love you?"

"You used to tell me that all the time." She stared up at him. "And then you left."

Harley gave her a gentle smile. "It was still the right thing to do."

"Yes," she admitted. "It was, but you shouldn't have stayed away so long."

"And that I'll give you full points on. I was a fool, and we have some time to make up for that."

She snuck her arms around his neck, pulled his head down to her. "Absolutely. I don't know how many times I tried to get you to make love to me before. How much trouble will it be to get you to do that now?"

He chuckled. "Absolutely none. I've been wanting the exact same thing since years before I left." He went to close the door, looked at her, and asked, "Are you okay with the dogs in or out?"

"Wherever they're comfortable."

He looked to see one lying outside Jimmy's door and the other one lying in the hallway. "It'll probably take them a while to get comfortable here, but we'll leave the door open."

She shook her head. "We can open it afterward, but I don't want the door open right now."

He smiled, nodded, and closed it on the dogs. As he turned around, she was already sitting on the bed, waiting for him.

"I can't believe it," she said. "I mean, not only do you just blast back into town, bringing havoc and chaos with you, but then you solve it all, and we're sitting here, just like we used to."

"True." He sat down beside her. "*Almost* like we used to."

She smiled, her hand going to where his arm was gone. "This is nothing. I don't have a problem with it at all."

"I'm glad to hear that," he said quietly, "because a lot of people would."

"Well, not me. I've loved all of you for a long time."

"And I knew it. I really did. Leaving back then was still the right thing to do."

She looked up, smiled at him. "No more excuses, it's time for us now."

He lowered his head and kissed her gently, tenderly.

She shook her head. "And I'm not breakable, and I'm not worried about what happened last time."

He frowned.

She shook her head. "That's the good thing about not remembering anything. So this will be the first time."

He smiled. "In that case, let's make it great." Wrapping his arm gently around her, he pulled her in, and he kissed her, gently deepening it until she was limp against him. Then she moaned, as he gently drifted kisses across her face and down her chin and her neck.

She stretched out on the bed and smiled. "I'm still dressed."

"We'll take care of that nighty in no time," he murmured.

And before she knew it, the light cotton material was up and over her head. She laughed in freedom and joy. "I feel so good to be here, with you."

He placed a finger against her lips and then replaced his finger with his passionate kisses, until she couldn't even speak. When she finally raised her head again, she was shuddering, her whole body trembling in joy. But he didn't stop there. He moved down her body, one inch at a time, exploring, tasting, caressing, until she was mindless jelly.

When she tried to stroke him, he shook his head and whispered, "Not this time. I've wanted you for too long. Don't you dare divert my attention."

"It's not about me," she murmured.

"This time it is." He slid two fingers down between her legs into the curls at the apex of her thighs. She gasped, her thighs widening as she opened up for him. But just when she thought he would settle there, he slid down and placed a kiss right at the heart of her. She cried out, her hips lifting, only to remember that her son slept close by, immediately throwing her hand across her mouth to stifle her cries, as Harley explored the most intimate part of her. When she came apart on the bed while he watched, she thought there'd never been anything so intimate in her life.

She widened her thighs, held up her arms, and ordered him, "Come to me. I've waited just as long for you."

He slid inside until he was home.

She stilled in wonder at the foreign sensation. No pain, just joy and a wonderous sense of rightness. As she wrapped her thighs around him and held him tight, he gasped and struggled for control. And then, still holding himself up on one arm, while braced on the stump, he started to move. She cried out in joy, as her body came apart again and again. When he finally collapsed beside her, she whispered, "You know it was definitely worth waiting for. Yet I think about all the years we've could have been doing this …"

"Don't think about it like that. Some things had to happen as they did. Now we just get to have the fun of making up for lost time."

She curled into his arm, wrapped herself up in him, and snuggled up close. "I can get behind that."

He kissed her gently. "So what do you think? Do you want to stay here, or do you want to move?"

"Why don't we just leave it for now and see how my mother is?" she asked. "The future doesn't have to be decided all at once."

"No, as long as I get to be a part of it with you and Jimmy."

She opened her eyes, stared at him in wonder. "Absolutely. I don't think I would survive if you decided to walk away again."

"As long as you're okay that I'm back, this is where I intend to stay."

She reached up, kissed him gently. "And this is where you belong."

EPILOGUE

BADGER SAT AT his desk across from Kyron Edgewater, who stared at him, somewhat angered.

"You want me to go after a dog? Did you hear me say that I didn't want to do K9 anymore?"

"I did. And her name is Beth." He looked over at Erick, who sat beside him, and Erick picked up the argument.

"We figured it's one of the reasons that you probably need to do this. We know how much you love dogs. We know how much you love that part of your life. And we figure some trauma's still there that you might need to heal."

"But you're not shrinks." Kyron felt his temper spike. "And I didn't sign up for therapy."

"Maybe not, but, at the same time, I'd like to think that there's room in your heart to help out another animal."

"What's wrong with it?"

"She's missing a leg, was injured and retired out in Colorado."

"So that sounds like what all of us are dealing with." He made a hand motion at the three of them. He had two artificial knee joints, a missing lower leg, rib, and kidney. Well, bits and pieces were left of that kidney. "It is what it is."

"Sure, and then somebody went to do a check on Beth and to make sure she was okay. At which point, the new owners admitted that she had gone missing somewhere in the night a few months ago."

He stopped and stared. "Why the hell would somebody steal the dog?"

"We're not exactly sure," Badger admitted. "They were having trouble with the dog. That she was a little more aggressive than anticipated, and they didn't know why. So, when she went missing, they weren't too upset. They weren't planning on telling anybody either. Nobody would have known except for the dog welfare check."

"And so now what then?"

"We want to make sure Beth is okay."

"Obviously she's not okay. She's gone missing. If she was getting aggressive, you also know there's a damn good chance that somebody took her out back and shot her."

Badger winced at that. "I hope not. We've had really good luck finding these animals and giving them a much better life. But if Colorado isn't a place you want to go and if Beth is one you can walk away from …"

He frowned at Badger. "That's a low blow."

"Of course it is." Badger half smiled. "We're a little desperate here. We need people who can handle dogs."

"Of course I can handle dogs. The reason I didn't want to go back in the K9 unit is, I couldn't handle the death."

"And that's justified," Badger said. "Not to mention that you're not the first person to bring up that point. I'm just looking for somebody to take a quick trip and to see if they can find Beth."

"She went missing months ago? You know there'll be no sign of her."

"Maybe not but we have to take a look, don't we?"

He groaned. "And of course this isn't a paid job, is it?"

"Would it make a difference to you if it was?"

"No." He sighed. "Just that you want somebody who can find this dog and make sure she's okay."

"Yes, and we'll cover the trip, and we'll cover the hotels and any equipment you might need." Badger studied him closely. "Are you okay with Colorado?"

"Sure. Why wouldn't I be okay with Colorado?" he asked in exasperation. "Aspen was my winter playground."

"And how will you handle returning there in the wintertime, when you only have one leg."

He glared at him. "Maybe I'll pick up snowboarding and see how that works."

"Maybe you should. For all we know, Beth's been taken into Search and Rescue and is just fine."

At that, Kyron shrugged. "You know that actually wouldn't be a bad field for her."

"Except for the missing leg."

"Possibly." He stared off in the distance. "Maybe a prosthetic could be made for her too."

"Why don't you go find Beth, then talk to Kat about that," Badger suggested, "but only if you're interested."

His glare deepened. "You know I'm interested. You also know there's no way in hell I'll leave that dog in trouble."

"That's what we figured," Badger noted in satisfaction. "Still, it's your choice."

"Meaning, you knew I would go." Kyron got up and walked outside. He stopped, took a deep breath, and he knew that he was in for headache and heartache.

Every time it seemed like he got around dogs, it was just bad news. They either got killed, taken away, injured, or something bad happened.

But this one was already injured, the other part of his

brain argued. *Maybe, this time, it'll go better for both of you.*

He doubted it. But he was a sucker for anyone in trouble. Especially a dog. "Hang on, Beth. I'm on my way."

This concludes Book 14 of The K9 Files: Harley.

Read about Kyron: The K9 Files, Book 15

THE K9 FILES: KYRON (BOOK #15)

Welcome to the all new K9 Files series reconnecting readers with the unforgettable men from SEALs of Steel in a new series of action packed, page turning romantic suspense that fans have come to expect from USA TODAY Bestselling author Dale Mayer. Pssst… you'll meet other favorite characters from SEALs of Honor and Heroes for Hire too!

Kyron swore he wouldn't work with dogs anymore, but, when Badger asks him to go home to Aspen and to track a missing War Dog, who is missing her left leg—as he is—Kyron can't refuse. Even if it means seeing his brother and his wife again. Not that he had anything against them. Kyron just couldn't deal with his parents. Finding the dog seems like the easiest part of returning to Aspen, until Kyron realizes a rescue run by a fascinating woman is the one that's spotted the missing dog, … only the dog isn't alone …

Miranda spends every waking moment working to keep her animals safe. Two jobs keeps them in food and shelter but not much more. Considering her miserable neighbor is always making complaints about her, she has considered moving, but it is too expensive to make that happen. She has seen a three-legged canine hanging around the back perimeter of her property and had been feeding it, quietly knowing it resembled the dog the neighbor had brought home, until it ran away.

She had no intention of letting her neighbor or anyone else know about the dog, hoping to coax it onto her property, where she could look after it properly. However, then Kyron showed up, searching for the animal, and things got really ugly …

Find Book 15 here!

To find out more visit Dale Mayer's website.

https://geni.us/DMKyronUniversal

Author's Note

Thank you for reading Harley: The K9 Files, Book 14! If you enjoyed the book, please take a moment and leave a short review.

Dear reader,

I love to hear from readers, and you can contact me at my website: www.dalemayer.com or at my Facebook author page. To be informed of new releases and special offers, sign up for my newsletter or follow me on BookBub. And if you are interested in joining Dale Mayer's Reader Group, here is the Facebook sign up page.
http://geni.us/DaleMayerFBGroup

Cheers,
Dale Mayer

About the Author

Dale Mayer is a *USA Today* best-selling author, best known for her SEALs military romances, her Psychic Visions series, and her Lovely Lethal Garden cozy series. Her contemporary romances are raw and full of passion and emotion (Broken But … Mending, Hathaway House series). Her thrillers will keep you guessing (Kate Morgan, By Death series), and her romantic comedies will keep you giggling (*It's a Dog's Life*, a stand-alone novella; and the Broken Protocols series, starring Charming Marvin, the cat).

Dale honors the stories that come to her—and some of them are crazy, break all the rules and cross multiple genres!

To go with her fiction, she also writes nonfiction in many different fields, with books available on résumé writing, companion gardening, and the US mortgage system. All her books are available in print and ebook format.

Connect with Dale Mayer Online

Dale's Website – www.dalemayer.com

Twitter – @DaleMayer

Facebook Page – geni.us/DaleMayerFBFanPage

Facebook Group – geni.us/DaleMayerFBGroup

BookBub – geni.us/DaleMayerBookbub

Instagram – geni.us/DaleMayerInstagram

Goodreads – geni.us/DaleMayerGoodreads

Newsletter – geni.us/DaleNews

Also by Dale Mayer

Published Adult Books:

Bullard's Battle

Ryland's Reach, Book 1
Cain's Cross, Book 2
Eton's Escape, Book 3
Garret's Gambit, Book 4
Kano's Keep, Book 5
Fallon's Flaw, Book 6
Quinn's Quest, Book 7
Bullard's Beauty, Book 8
Bullard's Best, Book 9

Terkel's Team

Damon's Deal, Book 1

Kate Morgan

Simon Says… Hide, Book 1

Hathaway House

Aaron, Book 1
Brock, Book 2
Cole, Book 3
Denton, Book 4
Elliot, Book 5
Finn, Book 6

Gregory, Book 7
Heath, Book 8
Iain, Book 9
Jaden, Book 10
Keith, Book 11
Lance, Book 12
Melissa, Book 13
Nash, Book 14
Owen, Book 15
Hathaway House, Books 1–3
Hathaway House, Books 4–6
Hathaway House, Books 7–9

The K9 Files

Ethan, Book 1
Pierce, Book 2
Zane, Book 3
Blaze, Book 4
Lucas, Book 5
Parker, Book 6
Carter, Book 7
Weston, Book 8
Greyson, Book 9
Rowan, Book 10
Caleb, Book 11
Kurt, Book 12
Tucker, Book 13
Harley, Book 14
Kyron, Book 15
The K9 Files, Books 1–2
The K9 Files, Books 3–4
The K9 Files, Books 5–6

The K9 Files, Books 7–8
The K9 Files, Books 9–10
The K9 Files, Books 11–12

Lovely Lethal Gardens

Arsenic in the Azaleas, Book 1
Bones in the Begonias, Book 2
Corpse in the Carnations, Book 3
Daggers in the Dahlias, Book 4
Evidence in the Echinacea, Book 5
Footprints in the Ferns, Book 6
Gun in the Gardenias, Book 7
Handcuffs in the Heather, Book 8
Ice Pick in the Ivy, Book 9
Jewels in the Juniper, Book 10
Killer in the Kiwis, Book 11
Lifeless in the Lilies, Book 12
Murder in the Marigolds, Book 13
Nabbed in the Nasturtiums, Book 14
Offed in the Orchids, Book 15
Lovely Lethal Gardens, Books 1–2
Lovely Lethal Gardens, Books 3–4
Lovely Lethal Gardens, Books 5–6
Lovely Lethal Gardens, Books 7–8
Lovely Lethal Gardens, Books 9–10

Psychic Vision Series

Tuesday's Child
Hide 'n Go Seek
Maddy's Floor
Garden of Sorrow
Knock Knock...

Rare Find
Eyes to the Soul
Now You See Her
Shattered
Into the Abyss
Seeds of Malice
Eye of the Falcon
Itsy-Bitsy Spider
Unmasked
Deep Beneath
From the Ashes
Stroke of Death
Ice Maiden
Snap, Crackle…
What If…
Psychic Visions Books 1–3
Psychic Visions Books 4–6
Psychic Visions Books 7–9

By Death Series

Touched by Death
Haunted by Death
Chilled by Death
By Death Books 1–3

Broken Protocols – Romantic Comedy Series

Cat's Meow
Cat's Pajamas
Cat's Cradle
Cat's Claus
Broken Protocols 1-4

Broken and... Mending

Skin
Scars
Scales (of Justice)
Broken but... Mending 1-3

Glory

Genesis
Tori
Celeste
Glory Trilogy

Biker Blues

Morgan: Biker Blues, Volume 1
Cash: Biker Blues, Volume 2

SEALs of Honor

Mason: SEALs of Honor, Book 1
Hawk: SEALs of Honor, Book 2
Dane: SEALs of Honor, Book 3
Swede: SEALs of Honor, Book 4
Shadow: SEALs of Honor, Book 5
Cooper: SEALs of Honor, Book 6
Markus: SEALs of Honor, Book 7
Evan: SEALs of Honor, Book 8
Mason's Wish: SEALs of Honor, Book 9
Chase: SEALs of Honor, Book 10
Brett: SEALs of Honor, Book 11
Devlin: SEALs of Honor, Book 12
Easton: SEALs of Honor, Book 13
Ryder: SEALs of Honor, Book 14
Macklin: SEALs of Honor, Book 15

Corey: SEALs of Honor, Book 16
Warrick: SEALs of Honor, Book 17
Tanner: SEALs of Honor, Book 18
Jackson: SEALs of Honor, Book 19
Kanen: SEALs of Honor, Book 20
Nelson: SEALs of Honor, Book 21
Taylor: SEALs of Honor, Book 22
Colton: SEALs of Honor, Book 23
Troy: SEALs of Honor, Book 24
Axel: SEALs of Honor, Book 25
Baylor: SEALs of Honor, Book 26
Hudson: SEALs of Honor, Book 27
Lachlan: SEALs of Honor, Book 28
SEALs of Honor, Books 1–3
SEALs of Honor, Books 4–6
SEALs of Honor, Books 7–10
SEALs of Honor, Books 11–13
SEALs of Honor, Books 14–16
SEALs of Honor, Books 17–19
SEALs of Honor, Books 20–22
SEALs of Honor, Books 23–25

Heroes for Hire

Levi's Legend: Heroes for Hire, Book 1
Stone's Surrender: Heroes for Hire, Book 2
Merk's Mistake: Heroes for Hire, Book 3
Rhodes's Reward: Heroes for Hire, Book 4
Flynn's Firecracker: Heroes for Hire, Book 5
Logan's Light: Heroes for Hire, Book 6
Harrison's Heart: Heroes for Hire, Book 7
Saul's Sweetheart: Heroes for Hire, Book 8
Dakota's Delight: Heroes for Hire, Book 9

Tyson's Treasure: Heroes for Hire, Book 10
Jace's Jewel: Heroes for Hire, Book 11
Rory's Rose: Heroes for Hire, Book 12
Brandon's Bliss: Heroes for Hire, Book 13
Liam's Lily: Heroes for Hire, Book 14
North's Nikki: Heroes for Hire, Book 15
Anders's Angel: Heroes for Hire, Book 16
Reyes's Raina: Heroes for Hire, Book 17
Dezi's Diamond: Heroes for Hire, Book 18
Vince's Vixen: Heroes for Hire, Book 19
Ice's Icing: Heroes for Hire, Book 20
Johan's Joy: Heroes for Hire, Book 21
Galen's Gemma: Heroes for Hire, Book 22
Zack's Zest: Heroes for Hire, Book 23
Bonaparte's Belle: Heroes for Hire, Book 24
Noah's Nemesis: Heroes for Hire, Book 25
Tomas's Trials: Heroes for Hire, Book 26
Heroes for Hire, Books 1–3
Heroes for Hire, Books 4–6
Heroes for Hire, Books 7–9
Heroes for Hire, Books 10–12
Heroes for Hire, Books 13–15
Heroes for Hire, Books 16–18
Heroes for Hire, Books 19–21
Heroes for Hire, Books 22–24

SEALs of Steel

Badger: SEALs of Steel, Book 1
Erick: SEALs of Steel, Book 2
Cade: SEALs of Steel, Book 3
Talon: SEALs of Steel, Book 4
Laszlo: SEALs of Steel, Book 5

Geir: SEALs of Steel, Book 6
Jager: SEALs of Steel, Book 7
The Final Reveal: SEALs of Steel, Book 8
SEALs of Steel, Books 1–4
SEALs of Steel, Books 5–8
SEALs of Steel, Books 1–8

The Mavericks

Kerrick, Book 1
Griffin, Book 2
Jax, Book 3
Beau, Book 4
Asher, Book 5
Ryker, Book 6
Miles, Book 7
Nico, Book 8
Keane, Book 9
Lennox, Book 10
Gavin, Book 11
Shane, Book 12
Diesel, Book 13
Jerricho, Book 14
Killian, Book 15
Hatch, Book 16
The Mavericks, Books 1–2
The Mavericks, Books 3–4
The Mavericks, Books 5–6
The Mavericks, Books 7–8
The Mavericks, Books 9–10
The Mavericks, Books 11–12

Collections

Dare to Be You…
Dare to Love…
Dare to be Strong…
RomanceX3

Standalone Novellas

It's a Dog's Life
Riana's Revenge
Second Chances

Published Young Adult Books:

Family Blood Ties Series

Vampire in Denial
Vampire in Distress
Vampire in Design
Vampire in Deceit
Vampire in Defiance
Vampire in Conflict
Vampire in Chaos
Vampire in Crisis
Vampire in Control
Vampire in Charge
Family Blood Ties Set 1–3
Family Blood Ties Set 1–5
Family Blood Ties Set 4–6
Family Blood Ties Set 7–9
Sian's Solution, A Family Blood Ties Series Prequel Novelette

Design series

Dangerous Designs
Deadly Designs
Darkest Designs
Design Series Trilogy

Standalone

In Cassie's Corner
Gem Stone (a Gemma Stone Mystery)
Time Thieves

Published Non-Fiction Books:

Career Essentials

Career Essentials: The Résumé
Career Essentials: The Cover Letter
Career Essentials: The Interview
Career Essentials: 3 in 1